Rosalind's Roots

A Sequel to *Charlie's Girl* and *Nellie's Girl*

MARY-HELEN & DANIEL FOXX

DRAYTONVLLE PUBLICATIONS

7541 West Corrine Drive

PEORIA, ARIZONA

Copyright © 2017 Mary-Helen & Daniel Foxx

Cover design © Ethan A. Foxx

All rights reserved.

ISBN: 978-0-9914515-4-8

Other Books

By Mary-Helen Foxx and Daniel Foxx

Charlie's Girl

Nellie's Girl

By Daniel Foxx

I Only Laugh When It Hurts

Four Stories of Christmas

A Book of Military Quotes

With Eddy W. Davison

Nathan Bedford Forrest: In Search of the Enigma

Rebel Refugees: The Confederate Exodus to Mexico

Their books are available for purchase at Amazon.com, where you can preview them and read customer reviews and other related information. The authors can also be found on Facebook. If you enjoy *Rosalind's Roots*, third and final installment of the Rosalind Matthews trilogy, please write a review and post it on Amazon.com.

CHAPTER ONE

Rosalind Matthews paid the cab fare and carried her bags up the front porch steps. The bus ride back from Florida had been long and exhausting. It felt as though she had been sitting in an orange crate for hours. Her back hurt and her legs ached from being cramped. What she needed now was a hot bath and time to relax.

She set her bags down and fished for the house keys, finally finding them at the bottom of her purse, and unlocked the front door. The mailbox mounted on the wall was full, so she pulled out the mail and tucked it under her arm. She opened the door and stepped inside her grandmother's house—her house.

As tired as she was, she carried her luggage across the threshold and set it down in the foyer. Without sifting through the stack of mail, she tossed it absently onto the hall table with a sigh. It could wait until after she had had a chance to unwind. She was barely functioning as it was.

Though she had only been away for a week, the house smelled musty to her. Mental note: open the windows and air the place out tomorrow.

The couch looked so inviting she sat down to remove her shoes and stretch her toes. Looking about the living room, she caught a whiff of her shoulder. Her blouse reeked of tobacco smoke that had filled the bus. That was enough motivation to spur her up the stairs and into the bathroom for a soak in the tub.

Her soft, cotton pajamas felt comfortable as she began to towel her brown hair dry. Her image in the dresser mirror reminded her of the Fourth of July evening when it had curled in ringlets after a swim in the river.

Rusty O'Connor and his mother Evelyn had insisted they liked it that way. It tingled when Rusty had wound a lock of her curls around his finger. She lay down on her bed, and was sound asleep within minutes.

Some time after eight o'clock something roused her. In her grogginess she couldn't quite place the source of the noise in the dark house.

There it was again. Someone was knocking at the front door.

She dragged herself out of bed and down the stairs, pulling on her bathrobe as she went. When she turned on the porch light, she recognized her neighbor, Muriel Dobson, peering through the door window.

Rosalind opened the door and greeted her sleepily, "Hi, Mrs. Dobson."

"Hello, Rosalind. I'm so glad you made it back safely." The middle-aged woman stepped past her to enter the house. "Did you have a nice trip?"

"Very nice, thank you." Rosalind yawned. "Oh, excuse me."

"Did you locate any of your mother's people down there?" Muriel fished curiously.

"No, there's nobody left. I did find some valuable records in the courthouse, but nothing about where they moved to in New Mexico."

"Oh, that's too bad," Muriel said sympathetically as she sank heavily onto the couch.

"We've been keepin' an eye on the house for you. Mark William even mowed the yard while you were gone," she said with pride. "Things have been so much better since he came back home."

Muriel gazed about the room sadly, remembering times with her best friend, Grace Matthews. "I still can't believe she's gone," she said with trembling voice.

As they reminisced, Rosalind found herself listening attentively, and comforting the woman rather than dwelling on her own grief. She knew her neighbor had very few friends other than her late grandmother. This adjustment was going to be very hard for her, even though her errant son had come back home.

As she tried to pay attention, Rosalind observed changes in her guest that she hadn't really noticed before. Muriel had long since given up on coloring her hair, and the wiry gray had regained control. Worry lines creased her brow reflecting years of battling with her headstrong son Mark William.

He had come along unexpectedly after his two sisters had grown up. Unfortunately, his birth was soon followed by the departure of Muriel's husband, who left her for a younger woman. Raising the little redheaded, freckled-faced imp alone had taken all her patience and then some.

Rosalind remembered how she had first made his acquaintance on the day she had arrived on the 4:50 from Atlanta. Muriel and her boy had driven Grace down to pick up her long lost granddaughter at the bus depot.

From the time they met, he had considered her his one and only friend. He was very territorial, and fiercely jealous of any others, especially her friends Hank and Emily who lived across the street.

As he reached adolescence his feelings for her intensified. When Rosalind struggled to keep their friendship intact, and declined his invitations to date, he felt spurned. He knew she had a crush on the handsome star athlete and scholar, Hank Watson. So, in revenge, he set his sights on Emily's introverted younger sister Carrie, with near disastrous results.

The poor girl had no idea why Mark William was hanging around. She knew that she was plain, not pretty like her sister Emily. Her stringy blond hair reached to her waist, and she tried to hide her eyes behind her ragged bangs. She was so shy she wouldn't even take the trash out to the street until after dark.

When he came over to the curb to introduce himself one evening, it startled her so badly that she noisily dropped the lid of the trashcan. He picked it up and replaced it on the can with a smile and walked away.

He showed up another day to help her pull weeds in the front yard without uttering a single word. He knew he needed to gain her trust much like he would have with a wounded animal. He also knew how much that would irritate the Watson family. And that was the whole point.

After a few weeks he gradually coaxed Carrie to meet him in her backyard after dark. She was bewildered and flattered by his kisses. But as he grew more demanding, she was frightened by his attempts to go further.

All this time, her family had no idea what was going on, and she was afraid to tell them. But when big brother Hank came home from college for Christmas, she tearfully confided in him. He was filled with anger and wanted to confront the guy, but Carrie begged him not to. She was afraid of the consequences once her protector returned to school. Hank had talked it over with Rosalind and asked her to keep an eye on his little sister for him, and to intervene with her friend Mark William if possible.

As it turned out, Carrie found the courage to confront her pursuer all on her own, and made it clear she wanted nothing more to do with him. He was furious, but he could see that he had lost the battle, and he stopped coming over.

Shortly after that he had begun to hang out with a rough crowd down at the bowling alley. In addition to his rebellious smoking, he took up drinking, a lot. This misbehavior infiltrated his home life to the dismay of his distraught mother. After several ugly, drunken confrontations, he had left town on his motorcycle for parts unknown. But he had come home for the funeral of Grace Matthews, the one person in town he respected.

୧ﻌ൶

Muriel was speaking again, drawing Rosalind back from her thoughts of the past.

"My daughter, Mary Louise, and her husband, Howard, have been talkin' of movin' up to North Carolina. Mary Louise and Teena, that's my oldest girl, have always been close, and Mary Louise would like to live closer to her. You knew Teena has lived up there for several years, didn't you?"

Rosalind nodded as she considered the news thoughtfully. "What about the furniture store? Would you sell it?"

"I'd leave that up to Howard. He has a good business sense. He's even talkin' about hirin' a full-time manager to run it until we all decide what to do."

"And what about you, Mrs. Dobson? Would you move up to there too?" Rosalind asked with concern.

Muriel wrinkled her brow before answering. "Howard bought some property near Hendersonville last year. They're thinkin' about buildin' a new home on it. Mary Louise wants him to include a mother-in-law addition for me. I guess that wouldn't be too bad," she finished sadly.

"Would Mark William go?"

Rosalind knew that he was dealing with an acute case of wanderlust. He might just pack up on his motorcycle and take off for new adventures at any time.

"I've been tellin' him he should think about joinin' the military service, not that he ever listens to a thing I say," she said with sarcasm. "I think it would be good for him, but he's become such a free spirit." Muriel shook her head at the notion of her boy having to take orders from anyone.

Rosalind's mind was wandering again. She momentarily lost track of the narrative as she remembered her past week in that most naval of households, the O'Connor family home in Adrian, Florida.

"I just don't know what I should do." Muriel paused, her head bowed in thought. "This has been our home for so many years, it would be hard to leave it. But there's not much else holdin' me here in Grayson. I guess I could rent it out. I don't want to sell it, you know. Maybe Mark William would want to live there again someday. Permanently, I mean." She smoothed out the skirt on her lap as she wished she could smooth out her life.

Muriel went on speaking as if she were talking to her dear friend, Grace. It was almost as if she were expecting Rosalind to tell her what to do. *Grace would have,* Muriel thought. *Or at least she would tell me if what I was sayin' made any sense.* But Rosalind was not Grace, and didn't have the experience and discernment of her grandmother.

It was going on nine o'clock when Muriel made the last of several overtures to leaving. Rosalind was looking forward to her departure, yet didn't want to seem rude. This time her neighbor actually began to rise stiffly from the couch.

"I suppose I should go on home and let you get some sleep. I know you must be worn out from your trip." She heaved herself the rest of the way up and made her way to the front door.

"Goodnight, Mrs. Dobson. Thanks for looking out for things for me."

"Goodnight, Rosalind." She hesitated, and then gave the girl a warm hug.

Rosalind returned the affection. "Say hello to Mark William for me."

"I will, honey."

After seeing her guest out, she dutifully picked up the stack of mail from the hall table to take upstairs with her. Yawning again, she stretched, and decided it would still keep until tomorrow. All she wanted to do now was to go back to sleep.

CHAPTER TWO

The sunlight awakened her at eight-thirty. Sleepily she looked around the room and realized that she had forgotten to set her alarm clock. Her brief vacation to Florida had postponed having to deal with living by herself. Now the quiet throughout the house reminded her how lonely and empty it was without her grandmother.

She dressed, put on her makeup and brushed out her hair. Then she picked up the stack of mail and sat down at the study desk that had once belonged to her dad.

The utility bills and the final statement from the funeral home went into the desk drawer. Then she sorted unopened sympathy cards into another pile. Reading them just didn't seem a good way to start her day. But the last one was postmarked Provo, Utah, a card from her friend Emily!

She reached for her letter opener and slit open the envelope. It was written on June 30th, before Rosalind had taken her trip to Florida:

> *Hi, Roz,*
> *It seems so long ago since we last saw*

each other at Christmas. I wish it had been a happier time for you.

Mom and Dad and the clan just moved into a nice new house and are all settled in. Dad likes his new job very much, and you know Mom, she would blossom wherever you planted her.

Carrie has been so much happier here in Utah. She has been dating some nice young men from the ward, and has been coming out of her shell.

Don is turning out to be a pretty good athlete, just like his big brother Hank.

Scott's turning twelve next month and will be ordained a deacon.

The twins Billy and Brent keep the family on their toes and in an uproar; and you wouldn't believe how big Brian has grown.

I'm dating someone new. The thing with the other guy didn't work out. Brad is from Idaho too, so it must be fate!

There are so many great chances to meet active, eligible bachelors out here that I can take my time and look around!

The big news is that Hank and Crystal are expecting a baby in January! It surprised us all. She had been feeling sick but they thought she just had the flu.

Roz, we were so sorry to hear about your sweet grandmother. You've been in my thoughts and prayers every day. I *know how much you must miss her. I'm sorry we weren't able to be there for the funeral.*

Wish you could come visit us. We would love to see you, and it would be good for you to be with those who love you.

Did you get the summer job at the library?

I know I've been terrible about writing, but I sure would like to hear from you.

Love always,

Emily

Rosalind returned the card to the envelope and stared at it for a while. She wondered how they had once been so close. Now it seemed that something more than distance was between them. With a sigh she put it into the stack of sympathy cards.

She shook her head as she tried to understand the strange mix of feelings she was experiencing. Then she stood in resignation and slowly walked out of her room.

On her way downstairs she remembered all the times she had answered her grandmother's voice calling from the kitchen to come down to breakfast. She wasn't very hungry. It was hard to be motivated to cook for just one person.

Just then a sudden taste for homemade waffles with jam seemed overwhelming. Brushing it aside to browse the kitchen cabinets and the top of the fridge, she found nothing that appealed to her. Another mental note: go grocery shopping.

She leaned against the doorframe leading from the kitchen to the foyer. Her luggage still sat there almost scolding her.

"Okay. Okay," she said as if they could hear her. She picked them up and climbed the stairs to her bedroom. This day seemed long already.

——

She opened her makeup case and removed her toiletries, makeup and hairbrush and put them away. She laid her suitcase on the bed and opened the latches. When she raised the lid, the first thing she saw laying there on top of her clothes was the manila envelope Rusty had given her at their parting. She had put it there inside for safekeeping after arriving at the Grayson bus depot.

She opened it and took out the 8 x 10 color photograph of her sitting behind Rusty on the beautiful chestnut mare, Sunny Girl, in the Fourth of July parade. That seemed so long ago. She studied his happy face and felt the warmth of his smile. She added to her mental shopping list: buy a picture frame.

Beneath it were her research notes from the Hillsborough County Courthouse. She thumbed through them briefly and stacked them neatly on a bookshelf beside her *Book of Remembrance*, a gift from Emily Watson that first Christmas here in Grayson.

As she began unpacking her clothes she was surprised to find Rusty's neatly folded, blue denim shirt she had worn in the parade. His mom had run a load of laundry and included hers, so she must have put it into her suitcase. *On purpose?* Holding it up to herself she looked in the mirror trying to imagine Rusty standing behind her.

Rusty O'Connor had entered her life on the first day of her Florida trip when she visited the Adrian newspaper office to begin her family research. She had never made a friend so easily. His smile was unforced and genuine, and disarmed her immediately.

When they sat on opposite sides of his desk in the office, she noticed for the first time that he nursed an injured leg. There was a prominent scar from above his eye to his cheek, and he had some damaged stubs of fingers on one hand. Noticing her stare, he quickly began to explain his injuries.

"I was serving with the Marine Corps in Vietnam when I got these. They don't bother me, and I don't want them to bother you."

Looking closely at the rodeo photo again, Rosalind touched his face. She hadn't realized how little she noticed his facial scar once she got to know him.

Rusty had taken Rosalind downstairs to search the newspaper's "morgue," where older issues were archived. From the beginning he seemed to take an interest in her quest for long lost family members, and supported her mission. Inexperienced as a traveler, she hadn't booked a hotel room for her stay, but Rusty saved the day.

"My folks run a bed and breakfast at our home. Right now they have no guests, so they have rooms available. That is, if you'd like to stay at the O'Connor hostelry while you're here."

It had proved to be the perfect arrangement. Rusty and the O'Connors had happily taken her into their family. They were very accommodating in Rosalind's search for her mother's family or any friends who might still live in the vicinity. Though her stay in Adrian had been brief, Rosalind had developed a strong affection for the three of them.

After beginning her new life at age fourteen with her grandmother in South Carolina, she had managed to compartmentalize her past experiences as a foster girl in Phoenix as the Arizona segment. Now, she realized she must create another compartment for the Florida trip. Grayson was her reality, her present.

The thought overwhelmed her with sadness as she hung Rusty's denim shirt on a coat hanger and placed it in the back of her closet. With a longing look at the handsome guy on horseback, she returned the photograph to the manila envelope and stuck it in the bottom drawer of her dresser. She was determined to close him out of her mind for now.

⸦⸧

The rest of the day was spent dusting, vacuuming and airing out the house. She would begin her summer job at the Grayson College Library in a matter of days, and realized she needed to do some mental housecleaning as well.

With regret she turned the knob and opened the door to her grandmother's room. She looked around, absorbing the essence that had been hers.

Grace's hairbrush lay on her dresser where she had left it. There were still a few strands of her long gray hair caught in the bristles. A faint scent of her favorite perfume lingered from the sachet packets in the dresser drawers.

In the corner stood a stack of empty boxes from the Piggly Wiggly grocery store. Thank goodness, Muriel had helped her bring them home in the trunk of her car before the Florida trip.

That reminded her: she needed to buy a car to maintain her independence, whether Mrs. Dobson moved away or not. Luckily, she had taken Driver Education in high school and had a valid learner's permit, although she had never taken the driving test nor gotten her license.

The memory of the Beast, as Rusty called his battered old blue pickup truck, came unbidden into her mind. She shuddered at the thought of almost having to drive it to Tampa to continue her research in the courthouse. Luckily, Rusty's dad had saved her from that fate by offering to drive her there.

She mulled over the idea of asking Muriel to help her practice her driving skills. Maybe she would even let her take the driving test in her old Ford.

As she sat down on the edge of her grandmother's bed to consider any other resources, her thoughts turned to the Grayson Ward congregation. The ward was fairly small, and although the members were friendly, she had not really made any close friends there since the Watson family had moved away.

She was sideswiped by another thought that intruded upon her. Her old crush, Hank Watson, was going to be a father! She knew he would be a good one, having learned from his dad's example.

She pictured Hank's face the last time she had seen him. That was the December when he had confided in her that he had fallen in love and was going to ask the girl to marry him. Even now, that triggered something deep inside. It surprised her that it still hurt so much to think of him.

With renewed determination, she stood and picked up a cardboard box and began packing shoes from the closet. Hats were next. She tried on one or two she liked, but decided against keeping any of them. Tears filled her eyes as she looked at the dresses still hanging there.

She turned away and tackled the dresser drawers instead. Everything was going to be donated to the Salvation Army; but the idea of someone else wearing her grandmother's dresses was too painful for the moment.

Grace Matthews hadn't worn much jewelry and was buried wearing her plain gold wedding band just as she had instructed in her last wishes. Her jewelry box on the top of the chest-of-drawers held a few pieces of costume jewelry that Rosalind had always admired. Those, she decided to keep. The rest she left to be given away.

Drawers were empty now, and packed boxes were piling up. Sorting Grace's things for give-away had been emotionally draining. She was physically tired as well. After carrying the last box down to the foyer, she decided to take a break.

She sat down at the old piano and began to play softly. There was no one there to hear her strike the occasional wrong note, so she increased the volume.

The strains of "Getting to Know You" from the musical, *The King and I,* brought back recollections of that night when she had accompanied Emily as she sang it in the Ward Talent Show. Sis. Watson was supposed to play for her daughter that night, but Emily's baby brother, Adam, had decided to come early.

Unaware that her fingers had stopped moving, Rosalind's mind played back wonderful memories of the Watson family. As these scenes faded before her, she steeled herself to go back upstairs to finish emptying her grandmother's closet. She also determined to write to Emily that night.

CHAPTER THREE

After rereading her answer to Emily's letter for the third time, she folded it, put it into an envelope, and sealed it with a sense of finality. The cobwebs of memory were beginning to part. She was finally able to accept the fact that Emily's brother Hank Watson would never be more than just a friend. That was beginning to make sense as she realized he had always really been more like a big brother. I'll cherish that, she thought. *I must be growing up.*

Trying to keep moving forward she listed things she most needed to get done before starting her summer job.

She had to get her driver's license, and she needed to buy a car. She felt totally inept at car shopping. She wished Mr. O'Connor were here to help. He felt like the closest thing she could remember to ever having a father.

However, she did have some acquaintances at church who might advise her. In fact, she had heard that one of the gentlemen sold insurance for a living. That might be a way to kill two birds with one stone.

The next thing on her to-do list was to write a note to the O'Connor family to thank them for their hospitality and friendship. And another one to thank Rusty. She dreaded writing that one because it might reopen the door to heartache.

The last thing on her list was to go over her research notes, and enter any new information on the long family group sheets and pedigree charts in her *Book of Remembrance*. Her grandmother Grace's death date and burial information had not yet been recorded in the Matthews Family Bible. She had a copy of the obituary and a memorial card from the funeral, and wanted to save them there as well.

She looked through her closet to see if any clothes needed pressing before starting to work. *Just keep busy.*

At bedtime the lyrics of a Johnny Mathis song came to mind for some reason. "Will I find my love today?" She hummed the melody and sang the last words "Or if I don't, I know tomorrow I will say, will I find my love today?"

∾∾

A couple of days later Brother Ken Phillips and his wife, Sandra, picked her up to help her find a car. Their third stop was the local Chevrolet dealership where Rosalind saw *the* car for her: an astro blue Chevy Malibu. It was a simple model, nothing extra special, just automatic transmission and an AM/FM radio. But it had air conditioning, a necessity for the hot, humid summers of the American Southeast.

She hadn't planned to buy a brand new model, but she had more than enough of the cash left over from Grace's life insurance. Brother Phillips, ever the great negotiator, got a good price for her. When she was offered a chance to test-drive, it she declined. She said she had done her research, and would accept Brother Phillips' final endorsement.

"Well, Rosalind, I think it's a good choice," he said. "If you like it, I would buy it."

The pleasant salesman shook hands first with Rosalind, then with Ken Phillips. "All we need to do now is write up this contract and a couple of other papers, and it's yours. While we're doing that, I'll have the lot boy run your car through the carwash to get the parking lot dust off it."

A short while later, the paperwork completed and signed, the salesman smiled. "Here are the keys to your new car, Miss Matthews. I hope it will serve you well."

As the three walked across the parking lot toward her new vehicle, Rosalind hesitated. "Brother Phillips, I guess I have the cart before the horse. I took Driver Education in high school, but my grandmother didn't own a car. I don't have my driver's license yet." She blushed. "Would you mind driving my car to my house, and let me ride with Sister Phillips?"

There was something in Ken Phillips' loud, friendly laugh that reminded Rosalind of Hank and Emily's father, Phil Watson. "No, I don't mind a bit driving this beauty. I'll tell you what," he said. "How about if we pick you up tomorrow during the lunch hour, and take you out for some practice. Then, when you feel ready, we'll drive you down to take the driving test."

"That would be wonderful! It doesn't make sense to let my new car just sit in the driveway," she joked.

"Alright then," he said. "You study up on the manual so you'll be ready to ace the test. I'll write up the car insurance policy for you, and you'll be all set."

The ride from the dealership to Rosalind's home took barely five minutes. After her friends drove away she proudly walked around her new Malibu and thought about her grandmother. *Would she approve?*

ა≫∾≪ა

Rosalind sat with a sheet of her best stationary before her and began a bread-and-butter note to her hosts, John and Evelyn O'Connor. Happy scenes danced across her mind as she relived each day of her trip.

The first time she saw Rusty she had been captivated by his striking blue eyes. After helping her research old newspapers, he took her out to dinner, where she watched him eat his French fries with mayonnaise and snitch "squiggly-loops", his term for fried clams, off her seafood platter. During her stay with his parents, each day started with hope and optimism like an unopened gift

John was a Navy veteran who had served in World War II and the Korean War. He was a little taller than his son and was in good physical condition for a man of his age. His hair was dark brown like Rusty's, but slightly gray at the temples. It was obvious how much they would have looked alike at Rusty's age.

Rusty's mother was shorter than her husband, who towered over her. Evelyn had a flawless complexion framed by her short, curly blonde hair. Rusty had inherited her clear blue eyes, but in all else, he resembled his father.

Rosalind eased back into her chair and laid down her pen as she remembered more. The highpoint of her trip had been Adrian's Fourth of July celebration. Her shoulders relaxed as the scenes of that day settled on her mind. The memories were real, but came to her almost as if in a dream. She could see herself riding in the rodeo parade.

In her reverie, she relaxed and felt safe and protected, just as she had that day riding behind Rusty. Perhaps it was out of that secure feeling that her affection for him had begun to grow. The daydream was so powerful that she could feel his arms holding hers close when she grasped his waist and leaned into his strong back.

The scene in her mind changed as if in a movie. She was back in that evening down at the river when he had asked to kiss her. Just a kiss, he had said. So sweet and gentle, yet thrilling, it had awakened new emotions within her, and left her hoping for more. But just as he had promised, he took her home instead.

When they did research together at the historical society, Rusty had stumbled across a shoebox of memorabilia not yet cataloged. Among the odds and ends was an old pocket watch that played "My Bonnie Lies Over the Ocean," Rosalind's long-remembered lullaby her mother used to sing to her. He had prevailed on the curator of the museum to allow Rosalind to take it home with her because it held such deep significance for her.

Now as she picked it up from her bedside table and opened it, the tune began to play, bringing back the joy she had known with Rusty as they shared the importance of the find, and their embrace that followed. She closed the watch and read the inscription on the back, "Together Forever."

This time, instead of bringing back that shared joy, the phrase brought back the unpleasantness between them as they had discussed the implications of marriage with someone not of her religion. Rusty had sensed the barrier growing between them. It clouded the happiness they could have enjoyed on her last two days in Florida.

Teardrops began to fall as she re-lived the pain of their parting, and the struggle she had had to honor her goal of a temple marriage. She laid her head down on the desk, and cried out her sorrow and hopelessness.

Eyes still wet, she raised her head and looked unhappily at the tear-stained sheet of stationary. Then she tore it into pieces. She would not write the O'Connors today.

❧❧

Monday July 16th was a bright summer day. Even before the alarm clock jangled its wake-up call, she was awake and lay quietly for a few moments looking up at the ceiling. Then she sat on the side of the bed, purposefully preparing for her first day of full-time work as the Assistant to the Librarian at Grayson College.

The outfit she had chosen the night before lay draped across the chair. It was a professional-looking, tan skirt and short-sleeved jacket with comfortable low heel shoes to match. To complete the look, she had chosen her grandmother's chalk white beads and matching, round, clip-on earrings.

Her breakfast of scrambled eggs, toast and orange juice was the perfect bracer she needed to clear her head. She checked her purse to make sure she had her new driver's license and car keys. Then she smiled and confidently stepped through the front door locking it behind her.

She walked around the side of the house to where her new car was parked. The previously neglected driveway had long since become a patch of lush, green grass, but now it would serve its purpose again.

She started the engine, backed out carefully, and set off for the college. It was a different Rosalind that went to work that day—a young woman who was focused and ready to face the next chapter of her life.

CHAPTER FOUR

August was nearly over. Students would be returning after Labor Day. The shipments of new books had been unpacked, accessioned, processed, and shelved on the book carts to be cataloged by the librarian upon her return.

Rosalind had registered for classes, bought her textbooks, and was looking forward to the fall semester with optimism. *Just keep busy.*

At the Grayson Ward, she was serving in the nursery, something she particularly enjoyed. There were not many young adults her age, and she sublimated her troubled feelings for Rusty by dishing out many hugs and having tender moments with these sweet little children. And they loved her back.

A letter arrived from Emily on September 1:

> *Dear Roz,*
>
> *I have great news.! I'm engaged! YES! I'm getting married, and I want you to be my maid of honor. Will you do it?*
>
> *Hank's wife Crystal is having a difficult pregnancy, and sure is sick a*

lot. He's going to be my Brad's best man. Happily their baby will be born before the wedding. He isn't much help right now because he's been busy helping Crystal.

Oh, did I mention that our wedding date is December 20th in the Salt Lake Temple? You'll be able to make it won't you?

Please write soon and tell me that you are coming. All the family is excited to see you again.

Love,
Emily

P.S.
Carrie and the rest of the family send their love. Mom and Dad say for you to fly out as early as you can so we can visit before we get busy with the wedding.

Rosalind laid the letter aside. It wasn't surprising that Emily was getting married. It was just another sign that their lives were growing farther apart.

However, the news gave her a lot to think about. She wasn't sure how she felt about making such a long trip alone. She had never even been in an airplane and was anxious about flying. There was also her apprehension about seeing Hank and Crystal.

Her feeling for him was still a scar buried somewhere deep in her heart. However, since their baby would be born by then, maybe that would make things easier. And it would be good to see all the Watsons again.

In October she was still fretting over her concerns about flying to Utah for Emily's wedding when, from out of the blue, she received another letter.

Rusty's mother, Evelyn O'Connor, was inviting her to come down to join them for Thanksgiving. Rosalind had mixed feelings about that, as well. The thought of seeing Rusty again filled her with unease and stirred up strong feelings.

Since her trip to Adrian, she had had no interest in dating anyone. Let alone a non-member of her church. But how would she find someone who would be able to take her to the temple to be married for time and all eternity? That had to be her focus. *Maybe Emily's Brad has a brother or a good friend.* She smiled at the thought.

As November approached and holiday decorations were everywhere, the prospect of being alone for Thanksgiving was just too much for Rosalind. So she wrote to accept Evelyn's kind invitation.

Conquering her anxiety, she called to reserve an airplane ticket from the Spartanburg-Greenville airport to Tampa. This could be a trial run before the longer flight to Salt Lake City in December.

Another letter arrived from Rusty's mom five days later. "We are all so excited that you're coming to spend Thanksgiving with us," she wrote. "Let us know as soon as you can what day you're coming, and what time your plane arrives, so we can be there to meet you."

Her letter didn't mention Rusty by name. There had been no mail from him since her return to Grayson last summer. That was not surprising, since she hadn't written to him either. Regardless of that, she really wanted to feel a part of the O'Connor family again, and was looking forward to the trip.

As she packed her bag, she pulled out the blue denim shirt from her closet. She pressed it to her face to smell the memories. If things had to be that way, she wanted to keep Rusty's friendship at least. She folded the shirt neatly and placed it in her suitcase so she could give it back to him.

On Wednesday before Thanksgiving, Rosalind drove her Malibu to the Spartanburg-Greenville airport. Several times along the way she reminded herself how far she had come, to be driving such a distance and taking a plane trip all by herself.

The signs confused her a couple of times as she looked for the passenger parking lot, but she found it on the third time around. It was a stiff walk to the entrance, and she was glad she had only brought the one bag and her makeup case.

Surprisingly, the terminal wasn't crowded, and she processed quickly at the airline desk checking her larger bag. Feeling embarrassed that she was such a beginner at this flying business, she leaned in close and in her best quiet voice, asked the attendant which way she should go to find her gate. The woman either didn't understand Rosalind's timidity, or didn't care, and loudly gave her directions while pointing the way.

Having arrived with plenty of time to spare before her flight, she picked up an abandoned newspaper on an empty seat, and sat down to read. When boarding was announced, she tried to blend in with the other travelers and appear as experienced as possible.

The airplane flight was so exhilarating she was almost disappointed to hear the captain announce that they were descending and would soon be on the ground in Tampa. Outside her window, she watched as the runway rose up closer and closer. The last few minutes before the wheels touched down were so exciting she was practically giddy with the thrill. As the plane taxied to a stop, Rosalind decided that between the two, the takeoff had been her favorite experience.

The airplane's door opened and passengers filled the aisle to deplane. Feeling like a seasoned traveler now, Rosalind moved along with the others and entered the terminal.

She looked around a little nervously as she noticed the other passengers happily joining up with their welcoming friends and loved ones. But as soon as she spied Mr. and Mrs. O'Connor, she waved and hurried to meet them.

John answered the unspoken question in Rosalind's eyes. "Rusty couldn't make it, but he'll join us later at home," he said reassuringly. She felt a mixture of disappointment and relief.

"Here, let me take your claim check. I'll go ahead to the baggage area and get your suitcase." He took a couple of steps and called back over his shoulder, "You only have one bag?"

"That's right."

"We're so happy you've come!" Evelyn said excitedly with an arm around Rosalind's waist. "You don't know how much we've missed you!" She gave her a squeeze, and Rosalind felt as though she had never been away.

⁓∘⌁

"Here we are. We made good time," John said as he pulled into the driveway of the O'Connor house.

Rosalind felt a sense of homecoming. It was exciting to see the front porch adorned with autumn décor. Her hostess pointed out the decoration on the front door.

"I made that fall wreath at a craft meeting," she said with pride.

"It's beautiful! You did a wonderful job," Rosalind said. "Your craft class has really paid off."

"Oh, it's not a class, exactly. A group of us ladies just got together at church." She didn't recall Rusty's mother being involved with a church.

John took Rosalind's bags to "her" room and returned to give her another hug. "It's so good to have you back, honey! You go ahead and settle in. Come on down to the den when you're ready."

Rosalind appreciated a few quiet moments alone to compose herself. Since this was going to be a short trip, she was traveling light, and there wasn't much to unpack.

She was already thinking ahead about her return flight on Sunday evening. That should give her plenty of time to attend church in the morning at least. She hoped that wouldn't be a problem for her hosts, or for Rusty.

A vase of fresh, fragrant flowers sat on the nightstand, which she assumed were from her thoughtful hostess. It was getting close to dinnertime, so she went down the hall to the kitchen to offer her help. She had just reached the foyer when the front door opened, and in walked Rusty smiling broadly.

"Hey, Rosalind," he said, as if they had just seen each

other the day before. He brushed off a little of the dust from his clothes and gave her a brotherly hug.

"Hello, Rusty." She smiled tentatively.

This was harder than she had thought it would be. His welcome was not really what she had looked forward to, but what did she expect?

"I apologize for my appearance, but I've been working on the river house, and I lost track of time. Give me a few minutes to get out of these work clothes and take a shower."

"We would all appreciate that," John quipped, from the den, fanning the air with his hand.

Rusty rolled his eyes at his dad. "I'll be back in a few minutes." He was gone as quickly as he had appeared.

His mother's expression gave no clue as to how things stood between Rosalind and Rusty. His dad had settled into his favorite chair in the den, not noticing how their reunion had gone.

❦

"I think we're ready." Evelyn called everyone to the dining room.

Rosalind smiled up at Rusty as he pulled out her chair for her. John helped Evelyn with hers, and they all sat down and clasped hands to say grace.

To no one's surprise but Rosalind's, Rusty offered the blessing on the food.

"Our Heavenly Father, we're so grateful for this opportunity to be together again, and for this food that's been prepared for us. Please bless it to our nourishment and strength, we pray, in the name of Thy Son, Jesus Christ. Amen."

"Amen," everyone chimed in.

Rosalind looked around the table in wonder, but no one seemed to notice anything unusual. Platters full of fried shrimp and French fries and a bowl of garden-fresh green beans were handed around. The talk for the next few minutes was of the menu.

Finally, Rusty glanced across the table at Rosalind. "How was your flight?" She noted that it was a different seating arrangement than last summer.

"It was sensational! Y'all probably didn't know this, but I'd never been on an airplane before. I didn't know if I would like it or not. But I really did! The takeoff was so thrilling! We went faster and faster, and then tipped upward, and I felt pushed back into my seat."

An amused John winked at his son.

"This first flight was kind of a test for me before I fly to Salt Lake City next month. I'm going out to be maid of honor at the wedding of an old friend of mine, Emily Watson."

"The girl who used to live across the street in Grayson?" Rusty asked with interest.

"Yes," Rosalind answered. She was surprised he would remember someone whose name she had only mentioned briefly on her last visit.

"Is she being married in the temple?" he asked as he speared a shrimp with his fork.

"Yes, in the Salt Lake Temple." She hoped it wasn't a sore subject.

"Then you'll only be able to go to the reception, right?" He kept his eyes on his plate.

"That's right." Rosalind answered softly, then abruptly changed the subject.

"Mrs. O'Connor, these shrimp are delicious! They're even better than those at the Colony Restaurant."

She grinned at Rusty. Everyone had a good laugh out of that. For the rest of the meal, nothing more was said about religion.

"Rusty, what time are Charlene and Russell coming over tomorrow morning?" John asked.

Rosalind looked up in surprise, first at John, and then at Rusty.

"Russell wants to watch the Thanksgiving parade on TV before they come over, so I told her to be here by 10:30. I knew Mom could use some extra help in the kitchen. As Confucius said, 'Many hands make light work,'" Rusty answered.

A stunned Rosalind waited for him to look her way, but he didn't. Evelyn was quick to explain.

"You met Charlene Stanford last summer. We thought it would be nice to include her and her son."

"Of course," Rosalind said. Hoping to cover any embarrassing reaction, she changed the subject.

"So tell me what all you're doing to the river house, Rusty."

"I hired someone to repair the roof. This week I fixed broken windows and put up new window screens. It's coming along, even if my bum leg does slow me up a bit."

Rosalind tried to catch Rusty's eye, but he seemed preoccupied.

"It certainly is a wonderful old place. Are you thinking of moving in when it's all finished?" she prodded.

"Maybe someday." Rusty looked up at her, and for a moment, she caught a tinge of sadness in his eyes.

Evelyn watched the awkward exchange and decided to intervene. "Who's ready for dessert?"

"Depends on what it is," John teased her.

"It's your favorite. Chocolate pudding," she said, patting him on the shoulder as she rose to go to the kitchen.

"Let me help you," Rosalind said and followed her, grateful for an excuse to leave the room.

Evelyn dished up the pudding. Rosalind added dollops of whipped cream in silence.

"I'm glad John and I have gotten to know Charlene. She's a very nice young woman," Evelyn said. "She took me to a craft day at her church last month. That's where I made the pinecone wreath."

"At a Relief Society work meeting?" Rosalind asked in surprise.

"Yes. They had a luncheon afterward, and I really enjoyed myself. There's another one next week, so I've signed up to try my hand at tole painting. I'm going to make a few Christmas ornaments."

Rosalind was beyond amazed, both at the news, and at the twinge of jealousy she felt. Seeing Rusty move forward with his life was not unexpected. On the other hand, having to share Evelyn's attention with Charlene was certainly a shock.

After dessert, John and Rusty went outside to sit on the porch. She helped clear the table, and as always, helped with the dishes.

"What have you been doing these past few months, Rosalind?" Evelyn inquired as she handed her a washed and rinsed platter to dry.

"Just working and going to school. Oh! and I bought a car! It's a blue Chevelle Malibu," she said proudly.

"That's wonderful! I know you'll really enjoy being independent and not have to catch rides all the time."

Rosalind knew it wasn't intended, but she felt another twinge. She remembered needing to be driven everywhere to do her research on her last trip down.

The kitchen cleaned up, and the table wiped, the ladies joined the men on the porch to enjoy the evening. Rusty was seated in the white wicker rocking chair, while John and Evelyn sat in the swing. That left the other wicker chair for her.

Probably better.

"How's the work on the porch and those steps going, son?" John asked.

"It's coming along," Rusty said. "At least I haven't stepped through any loose floorboards lately." He laughed, and Rosalind drank in the sound.

"When do you think it will be finished," she asked.

Rusty studied his blistered palms and took his time answering. "Not too much longer, I hope. Maybe by spring. It all depends."

"He's taking his time," Evelyn said proudly. "He wants it to be a real showplace like it used to be."

Rusty was still avoiding Rosalind's gaze. The squeaking chains on the porch swing filled the silence.

So much left unsaid. Was he fixing the place up for him and Charlene?

Some time later, Evelyn climbed out of the swing and said, "I'd better get to bed. I have to get up early tomorrow so I can get the turkey in the oven." She reached down to hug Rosalind where she sat.

"I'd probably better do the same," she said, not wanting to be left behind. "Goodnight." She smiled at John and Rusty who rose from their seats as the ladies went inside.

The men stayed up for a couple of hours talking football in the darkness while Rosalind lay awake in her bed battling her feelings and suddenly dreading the next day. It might bring answers she didn't want to know.

CHAPTER FIVE

When the morning sun broke early through the ruffled curtains, Rosalind squinted as though it were the enemy. She was dismayed to discover how much she was still dreading this day, the day that should be so happy.

The O'Connors had made her feel very much at home. Still, she just couldn't shake the feeling that something was not right. It was like an undercurrent she couldn't identify. Though it was almost palpable, she determined not to give in to it, at least for now. She certainly didn't want to draw any unwarranted conclusions, especially where Rusty was concerned.

Evelyn was scurrying about in the kitchen and made excuses about the quick and easy breakfast of cereal and milk, fruit juice and toast. Several items on the Thanksgiving menu were in various stages of preparation, and the turkey was roasting in the oven. She seemed more preoccupied than usual.

No one else was around, so after eating breakfast alone, Rosalind excused herself to wander out back to the patio where she could be out of the way for awhile. She took a seat in the glider.

There were a few toy cars and stuffed animals strewn across the lawn. She heard the back door open and looked around to see John stepping outside.

"It's nice to have a little one around again," he said as he began picking up the toys and putting them in a basket. "Russell looks just like his dad at that age. Geordie and Rusty had been friends from the time they were little."

Rosalind smiled wanly and wondered how long before Geordie's widow and son would arrive. She stole a glance at her wristwatch. It was only nine-thirty.

She hadn't seen Rusty all morning. *Maybe he's avoiding me.*

She tried to make polite conversation with John, but he seemed more reserved than usual. Everyone was dancing around what was really on her mind, if not theirs as well.

After a few minutes, she excused herself and went back into the house. With nothing to do, she headed toward the front porch.

Through the screen door, she saw Rusty sitting in the cab of his faded blue pickup truck, staring off into space. She stayed just out of sight and watched him until he got out of the truck and headed toward the porch. She debated whether she should linger and talk to him or not. It might be her only chance before the other guests arrived.

When he climbed up the steps and opened the screen door, he looked up into her face, startled to see her there.

"Good morning," he said with some embarrassment. "Happy Thanksgiving."

"Happy Thanksgiving to you, Rusty," she said with a smile. "How have you been?"

"Okay, how about you?" he asked noncommittally. "Have a seat."

Rosalind chose the wicker rocker and he took the one across from her as she thought of how to respond.

"To tell the truth, living alone has been a rough adjustment," she said honestly. "I think I'm doing pretty well though, all things considered.

"When I went back home in July, I boxed up all my grandmother's things and gave them away. That was harder than I'd thought it would be.

"I kept busy running the library the rest of the summer, and before I knew it, the new semester was beginning. I was able to arrange my work schedule so I could carry a full class load to stay on track for graduation."

"That's good," Rusty nodded, but that wasn't really what was on his mind.

"How are you doing now? Are you seeing anyone?"

"No," she answered matter-of-factly. "How about you?"

There it was. The question was hanging there between them. Rusty looked aside and seemed troubled as he considered what to say.

"I know what you're thinking, but I've been spending time with Charlene and Russell mostly for his sake. A boy needs a father figure in his life. It's the least I can do for Geordie." His voice trailed off and he seemed a little uncomfortable.

"Is that the real reason why you're fixing up the river house?" she probed.

"Maybe," he muttered. "Or maybe I just needed to feel like I was making some progress in my life. I'm not getting any younger, you know!" he joked sarcastically.

She studied his face intently. The twinkle she had so enjoyed was gone from his eyes. It had been replaced by an earnest seeking for something he was missing. Gone, too, was the easy way they could be close though across the room from each other. It was obvious he had moved on after her rejection last summer.

That came as a painful realization. She missed his touch on her shoulder as he passed her chair, or the hand that reached for hers under the table at mealtime.

She wanted to let him know, somehow, what she was feeling. But she couldn't find the right words.

Did she even know what her feelings were?

Has anything really changed?

As uncomfortable as things were now, she still felt she had chosen the right path.

A station wagon pulled up in front of the house, and the driver honked the horn. Charlene climbed out and her son scrambled across the seat to follow.

Her long blond hair was pinned up into an attractive figure eight. Rosalind was struck by how pretty she was with her peaches and cream complexion.

I hadn't remembered that.

"They're here!" Rusty called back into the house.

Is he happy for their arrival, or just relieved for a timely interruption?

Rusty's dad came out to greet the pair. Evelyn followed and stood by the door drying her hands on her apron. John scooped Russell up and swung him onto his shoulders.

"Hello," Charlene greeted everyone warmly. Then she turned to Rusty and gave him a peck on the cheek. Facing Rosalind, she shook her hand. "It's so great that you could come down to join us for the holiday."

"It's nice to see you again, Charlene, and you, Russell," she reached out to tickle the boy's ribs.

"Well, come on inside everybody," Evelyn called. "Charlene, honey, do you need help carrying anything in from the car?"

"No, thanks. Rusty can get it," she said. "Sweetie, there's a box of goodies on the back seat."

"Okay," he said.

Rosalind was still reeling from the proprietary kiss Charlene had given Rusty. She felt that sharp twinge again when she heard Evelyn use her own term of endearment for someone else.

This is going to be a very difficult day.

Hopefully no one was the wiser. She'd have to be extra careful to conceal her feelings.

John lifted Russell down from his shoulders. "Come on, young man, let's go out back and play catch with Rusty. We'll be in the back yard," he called to the ladies in the kitchen. "We'll stay out of the way so y'all can visit and cook."

The boy ran down the hall and out the screened back door. John caught it before it banged shut, and held it open for his son.

Charlene sat down at the small kitchen table. "Your Thanksgiving wreath turned out great," she complimented. "I'm lookin' forward to the tole paintin', aren't you?"

"Yes, I am. I've always admired it, and never have taken the time to learn how to do it. John tells me I couldn't paint the broad side of a barn," she joked.

"Do you have any favorite crafts or hobbies, Rosalind?" Charlene asked politely.

"No. I've been so busy with work and classes that I haven't been able to attend Relief Society during the week."

"What church callin' do you have in your ward?" Charlene pursued.

"I'm in the nursery," Rosalind said with a smile.

"Oh, I had that callin' for awhile before Russell started in Primary. Now I'm the Sunbeams teacher. Sometimes I wonder when I'll get to attend a regular class where I can talk with the grownups again," she said with a laugh.

Rosalind found herself relaxing and actually enjoying the conversation. She tried hard not to think of Charlene as the competition. She was a genuinely nice person. Rusty was lucky to have such a friend. *A friend or more?* She tried to put the thought out of her mind.

"Dinner won't be ready until about two o'clock," Evelyn said. "Why don't you girls take these crackers and cheese out to the patio."

The game of catch was abandoned as soon as Rosalind and Charlene put the trays on the patio table. The menfolk swarmed over the snacks.

"This little guy has quite an arm," John said as he rubbed the boy's head with genuine affection.

"Just like my daddy, right?" Russell smiled broadly, his mouth full of crackers.

"Right!" Rusty grinned approvingly.

That was his first real smile that Rosalind had seen since her arrival. She could tell that this relationship was filling a void in him, the need to look after his friend's boy and be his pal.

Or his dad?

It was going on noon when Evelyn called everyone in. "It's still a couple of hours before dinner. Why don't y'all drive out to see the improvements at the river house? I'll stay here and keep an eye on the stove. And Russell can be my helper," she said as she put her arm around the boy.

Rusty was about to object, but Charlene spoke up excitedly. "That's a wonderful idea! We haven't been out there for a couple of weeks. I'd love to see how it's comin' along!"

Rosalind was about to make her excuses to stay and help Evelyn with the cooking when Rusty glanced up at her. An uneasy look in his eyes caught her attention.

Soon, John was driving them down the river road, with the ladies in the back seat, and Rusty riding shotgun. Charlene made continuous conversation over the front seat with John and Rusty, while Rosalind tried to follow along. She didn't know any of the people they were discussing, and only really paid attention when Rusty spoke.

The old house came into view where the river road curved. Rosalind was amazed at the transformation, but Charlene was ecstatic.

"Oh, Rusty, you're doin' such a great job! It looks so much better already! It's really comin' along!"

The four of them got out of the car. They walked around the outside of the house picking their way through tall patches of sandspurs as Charlene chattered on.

"Have you thought any more about paintin' it a bright sunny yellow with navy shutters, instead of just plain old white?" she asked somewhat critically.

"No. I said I'd consider it. I haven't made up my mind yet." He glanced at Rosalind.

John walked ahead, drawing Charlene along to point out places that needed a woman's touch. Rusty trailed behind silently with his head down. Rosalind dropped back to keep him company.

"It's not my place to say anything, Rusty. But I thought a restoration was more what you had in mind, wasn't it?" she asked softly.

"Yeah, I guess so," he said glumly.

"Well, as a good friend once told me, 'Then you should have it. And don't let anything or anyone deprive you of that.'"

She stopped and faced him. John and Charlene had disappeared around the corner of the house. She took his hand and gazed directly at him until he looked up at her.

They stood that way in silence until they heard the others returning. Rusty quickly released her hand before they came into view. The look in his eyes became unreadable again.

"I guess we should be getting back," John said. "Why don't you ride up front with me, Charlene? I'd like to hear more about your suggestions for adding another bathroom off the back porch."

Rusty strode ahead and opened the back door for Rosalind, but Charlene got there first. She linked her arm through his and declined John's suggestion.

"I'll sit back here with my guy, if you don't mind, John."

A stunned Rosalind stared at the couple. Then, without a word, she looked away and walked around to the front passenger door.

John's clinched jaw betrayed his annoyance as he opened the car door for her. Once he had climbed behind the steering wheel and started the engine, he covered Rosalind's hand with his own. She grasped it and squeezed it with gratitude, smiling across at him. He winked at her encouragingly as he pulled out onto the river road.

❦

Back at the house in town, they were greeted with the rich aroma of Thanksgiving. The table was set, and Rosalind began carrying in the food to the dining room.

Charlene was in the den with Rusty, sitting on the arm of his chair, her arm around his shoulder. Russell had climbed into his lap.

Rosalind glanced at the three of them, and quickly turned back to the kitchen. Evelyn gave her a comforting pat on the shoulder, but said nothing.

They all gathered around the dining room table, reading the place cards to find their seats. Evelyn had placed Rusty and Rosalind next to each other, which was upsetting to

Charlene. She pouted a moment, and then sat across from them with Russell beside her.

Before they bowed their heads for the blessing, Evelyn squeezed the young mother's hand, and said, "I'm so glad you and Russell could join us today."

Rusty and Rosalind clasped hands and then reached out to the others. She treasured their moment of closeness as John bowed his head to pray.

"Oh Lord, on this special day, we thank Thee for more than this food. While we are grateful for it, we're also most grateful for Thy abundant blessings in our lives. We thank Thee that we can be together again. May each of us recognize the gifts Thou hast given us. Father, we're thankful for our forebears and their will and courage that brought them to this land, and that we have inherited their vision, and their contributions to this great country. We're grateful for all Thy blessings to us and for this food today."

There was a short pause and then John said, "Amen." He looked directly at Rosalind and smiled affectionately.

"Amen," the others said in unison.

Charlene looked up hoping to catch Rusty's gaze. She smiled her love and gratitude for him. He smiled back and reluctantly released Rosalind's hand.

Throughout the meal Rosalind was lost in her own thoughts. She tried to ignore the interactions between Charlene and Rusty. In an effort to avoid any more discomfort, he focused his attention on young Russell. Meanwhile, Evelyn and John tried to pick up any slack in the conversation.

"Do you have tomorrow off, Charlene?" John asked as he smiled politely.

"No. I have to work. I have the early shift, though. My mom is goin' to keep Russell tonight so I can come home and sleep after I get off. I have to work Saturday, too," she said sourly.

"That's good," said Evelyn, and then recovered by continuing, "at least you'll get a little rest before Sunday."

Evelyn turned her attention to her son, and said sweetly, "Rusty, I know you'll be taking Rosalind to church Sunday morning, but I'd really like you to come right back afterward so we can spend more time together before her flight."

"Sure, Mom," he agreed pleasantly, catching the hint.

Charlene reacted with surprise, and not a little displeasure. She flashed Rusty a determined look and said, "Oh, I thought we'd have lunch at my place after Sunday School, and then go back to church in the evenin'. You could drop Rosalind off early at the airport so you wouldn't have to miss Sacrament meetin'."

John looked at his plate with studied composure. Evelyn had already thought it through, and drove her point home.

"We get to see so little of Rosalind, we'd really like to spend that time together. You understand, don't you, honey?"

There it was again.

But this time, her addressing Charlene as "honey" didn't seem to pain Rosalind as much. She was in awe of the tactful way her gracious hostess had of handling delicate matters like these.

When Charlene realized she was pushing her luck, she gave in and tried to be polite about it. "Oh, of course, Evelyn. And we can see each other next weekend, right Sweetie?" she emphasized.

"Sure we can, Charlene," he said with a slight grin. "I promised to play ball with my buddy here."

Russell beamed at the prospect.

"And you'll come over and help us put up the Christmas tree too, won't you?" she pressed him.

"I'll be glad to."

Then Evelyn spoke up. "And don't forget, Honey, I'll be over for the craft meeting," Evelyn reassured her.

John smiled at his wife's ability to gently manipulate Charlene and smooth her ruffled feathers. She had worked that magic on him on more than one occasion, he admitted to himself.

After dessert, Charlene made a half-hearted offer to help with the dishes, reminding everyone that they were due back at her mother's house in Tampa shortly. So Rosalind took over the kitchen duties to give her more time with Rusty before they had to leave.

While Russell was vying with his mother for his idol's attention, John made no effort to intervene. Instead, he reclined in his chair to take a nap. As Rosalind passed by the doorway with a load of dishes, he opened one eye to give her a wink.

Finally, it was time for the Stanfords to leave. Evelyn packed up several containers of leftovers for them, which John carried out to her car.

"Thanks for a wonderful Thanksgiving, you two. We'll have to do it again next year, maybe out at the river house. And Rosalind, I guess I'll see you Sunday."

Rusty gave his namesake a piggyback ride to the station wagon, and deposited him in the front passenger seat. Then he walked around to the driver's side where Charlene waited.

As he opened and held the door for her, she grasped his shoulders and drew him in closer. The others watched in shock as she gave him a long, passionate kiss.

There was a hesitant response from Rusty. He clumsily put his hands on Charlene's waist, but seemed uncomfortable embracing her. After what seemed like an eternity, he stepped back and took her hand to help her into the car. Then he closed the car door firmly, and stood there red-faced, waving goodbye as she drove off.

Rosalind fled to her room to avoid seeing anyone. John and Evelyn, who had watched the distressing scene from the porch, now hurried back inside.

"I don't know what to think." Evelyn was upset. "I knew Rusty was spending a lot of time with them, but I thought it was just for the boy's sake, and that they were just good friends. I had no idea things had gotten to this point." She shook her head in dismay. "With Rosalind here, I certainly wouldn't have invited them today if I had known."

Maybe his wife had just been too busy or naïve to notice the growing relationship, but John knew better. Striding down the hall, he muttered angrily.

"What was that woman thinking, making a public display like that in front of all of us? You know what a private person Rusty is! He must have been mortified!"

"Keep your voice down, John," Evelyn pleaded. "You don't want Rosalind to hear you. She must have been humiliated!"

"He needs to get his head on straight, and soon, before he loses her!" His voice trailed off as he closed their bedroom door.

Rosalind lay on her bed. Her chest felt tight and her eyes burned as she struggled to hold back her emotions. But hot tears escaped, flowing down her cheeks to wet her pillow.

Poor Rusty! I feel so bad for him. It wasn't his fault.

She heard the front door open and close loudly. The sound of the TV blared from the den when Rusty tuned in another football game. Even his solitary shouts of complaint and cheers of victory could not keep Rosalind awake. She slept soundly until after five o'clock.

CHAPTER SIX

Rosalind became aware of someone standing beside her bed, patting her hand softly.

"I'm sorry to wake you, honey. Rusty is so embarrassed. He feels so bad about what happened earlier," she said sadly. "I hope you're not too upset with him."

"No. Of course not," Rosalind reassured her.

"Well, anyway, he's going out to the nursing home to see Bob Owens, and he wondered if you'd like to go."

Rosalind looked up into Evelyn's kind face and smiled. "I certainly would. Thank you."

She always avoided addressing Rusty's mother by name. It just didn't seem respectful to call her by her given name, as Charlene did. But the name that readily came to mind, "mom," would seem way too presumptuous. Instead, she climbed out of the bed and gave her a warm hug.

"You two can stay as long as you like. Everyone's probably too stuffed to eat supper yet. We'll just have turkey sandwiches and leftovers when you get back."

Rusty was pacing quietly in the hall. He waited nervously while she brushed her teeth, spruced up,, and applied fresh makeup.

"Ready to go?" he asked sheepishly as she stepped through the door.

"I sure am," she responded warmly. "I'm so glad you invited me."

Visibly relieved, Rusty said, "I haven't been out to visit Bob enough lately. I just let other things get in the way," he admitted. "Anyway, today seems like a good time to look in on him."

Rosalind smiled her approval and followed him as they headed out to his truck.

"Ah, the Beast! How I've missed you!"

She patted the dashboard with affection as she climbed up into the cab. Rusty grinned one of his best, and lingered at the door after he closed it, enjoying the sight of her sitting there.

As they drove off she asked, "How's Miss Leonard coming along with the museum?"

"She's almost ready to open it to the public, probably next spring. She finally tattled on me, and I had to cave in, and promise to take my military portrait down there for her wall of 'fame'."

Rosalind laughed and slapped his hand lightly as it rested on his thigh. He grasped hers before she could remove it, and they enjoyed the ride in silence. Things were good.

Rusty rested his hand on Rosalind's shoulder as they made their way through the lobby to the front desk of the rest home. The young receptionist recognized the handsome guy in the Marine Corps baseball cap, and smiled as they approached.

"Hi. Happy Thanksgiving," Rusty said cheerfully.

"Happy Thanksgiving to you, too."

"Thanks. It's been a good one," he said with a glance toward Rosalind. "We're here to see Bob Owens."

She offered the guest book with a flirtatious smile. Ignoring her obvious attentions, Rusty signed them both in as Rosalind covered her amusement.

They looked around for Bob in the recreation room, but he wasn't there. Rusty spoke to several of the other veterans as he escorted Rosalind down the hall to his friend's door.

It was almost twilight and the room was dimly lit. The elderly man lying there perked up at their entrance, and tried to sit up a little straighter.

"Here, Bob. Let me raise that up a bit for you," Rusty offered.

He grabbed the crank at the foot of the old hospital bed and began to turn it. The head of the bed complained noisily as it slowly raised Bob into a reclining position. He seemed to be much more frail than the last time Rusty had seen him.

"How's that feel now, buddy?" Rusty asked.

"That's just right," Bob said. "It's sure good to see you, Marine. How's your Thanksgiving been?"

Rusty grinned as he nodded toward Rosalind. "Our special guest here has made it pretty terrific."

"Hey there, young lady. You're looking even prettier than the last time I saw you. You sure know how to pick 'em, Rusty." Bob smiled an almost toothless grin.

"How are you, Bob?" Rosalind leaned down to give him a hug. "It's nice to see you again."

The curtain was drawn separating Bob's half of the room from that of his roommate. They could hear a soft voice on the other side.

"He's not doing too well," Bob said quietly. "They tried to find any family. Then just this week, they turned up his daughter. That's her with him now. I guess they've been out of touch for years. It must have been kind of a shock to her, getting a call like that."

"Do you think maybe we should go down to the rec room and give them some privacy?" Rusty asked with concern as he glanced around for a wheelchair.

"No. I really don't feel up to it right now."

Bob shifted his position to ease the pressure on his hips. He seemed depressed, and not his usual cheery self. His roommate's terminal condition was weighing heavily on him.

A nurse passed through the room on her way to check on the failing patient. As she drew back the curtain, they could see him lying there, looking very pale. His breathing was shallow and labored. His eyes were locked on the ceiling. As the nurse stepped back out of the room, the shake of her head conveyed that he was failing fast.

Seated beside him, with her back to the curtain, was the daughter visiting Bob's dying roommate. Her shoulders shook with silent sobs. Rosalind wished she could do something to comfort her, but felt helpless.

"Music's the only thing that seems to reach him," Bob said softly. "Back when I was first admitted here, a nurse told me he had severe brain damage from the big war. He couldn't talk. He couldn't communicate at all." Bob shook his head sadly. "He's been here a lot longer than I have, and this is the first time he's had any visitors that I know of. Too bad. Now it's almost too late."

Rusty looked on the scene with compassion, and put his arm around Rosalind's waist. Her gaze was fixed on the dying man with the full shock of white hair and a blank expression upon his face.

Moments later the nurse returned to check his vitals, and left without a word to the grieving visitor. She tossed a whispered comment to Bob on her way out, "It won't be long now."

"He likes music," Bob answered, but by then she was already headed out the door again and didn't hear him.

Rosalind's heart ached with sadness for this woman sitting with her long-lost father. It brought back memories of the hours she had spent beside her comatose grandmother's bedside after her fall down the attic stairs. She unconsciously began humming, "My Bonnie Lies Over the Ocean."

Remembering the pocket watch she always carried with her, she reached into her purse and took it out. Standing close to the curtain, just out of sight, she wound the watch, and opened it. The tinkling sound of the music box came to life and played its melody.

The dying man's eyes seemed to come into focus as he listened for a moment. Then he turned his head slightly in the direction of the sound. His daughter sat upright, and looked over her shoulder in confusion, to see where the music was coming from. Then she turned back to observe the change in her father. His eyes still stared toward the sound. Then he raised his hand as if to catch the elusive notes from the air.

Rosalind glanced at her for approval, and stepped forward through the curtain. She held up the pocket watch to show him.

"Together forever," she read the inscription. Then she closed the watch and placed it in his reaching hand.

He pressed it to his cheek. With great effort, his lips moved, and though it came out as a hoarse whisper, the word was unmistakable. "Bonnie."

He looked up into Rosalind's face as though he recognized her. An almost undetectable smile came to his eyes.

"Nellie?"

Then he looked at the woman seated beside him.

"Susie?"

With tears rising in his eyes, he spoke again.

"My girls!"

In that moment, Rosalind realized why she had felt such compassion toward the old veteran. Even if he had not uttered his daughters' names, she knew. This man who had broken his silence of years was her grandfather. She felt in her heart that she had become part of an exquisite miracle.

After a few brief seconds, his hand still grasping his pocket watch, his lips spread into a smile. He stared off at the familiar flower on the wallpaper, and crossed over peacefully.

CHAPTER SEVEN

The room seemed filled with peace. Everyone felt overcome by the loveliness of the scene. Bob's lips quivered as tears flowed down the hardened veteran's weathered cheeks. Rusty moved closer to comfort his old friend.

Rosalind spoke softly, "Aunt Sue? My name is Rosalind Matthews. I'm Nellie's daughter," she said gently.

The woman stood and turned in amazement. A look of confusion crossed her face.

"You're Nellie's girl? My sister had a daughter?"

"Yes," Rosalind answered. "I'm Charlie Matthews' girl, and Nellie was my mother."

Sue put her hand to her cheek and studied the face of the girl before her. "It's true! The resemblance is remarkable!" She opened her arms and clasped Rosalind to her.

"I never knew what happened to my sister after we lost touch all those years ago." She held her niece at arm's length. "We have a lot to catch up on." She stepped back, wiping her eyes with the damp, crumpled handkerchief in her hand, and smiled.

Sue turned to look at her father's face, trying to see in him the strong young daddy she had known. She smoothed his white hair into place, but couldn't bring herself to close his partly opened eyes. He seemed so happy and at peace.

What was he seeing? Rosalind wondered. She gently opened his hand, and retrieved the treasured pocket watch.

Just then the nurse came back into the room cutting their reunion short. "Pardon me," she said quietly. "The attending physician is on his way."

She had barely said it when the doctor entered the room. He examined the patient, took his pulse, listened with his stethoscope, and declared him deceased. Then he reached out to close his eyes, and drew the sheet over his face slowly, and with great respect.

"I'm very sorry. I'm just so glad we were able to contact you so you could see your father again," he said to Sue as he shook her hand.

Rusty stepped up, calling on his background of experience with wartime deaths. "He came to just before he died, Doc. He seemed to recognize his family."

"Thanks for telling me. That's a blessing. I've been his doctor for over six years. I wish I'd been here for that," the physician said earnestly.

Sue wiped her eyes and spoke up. "It's a day for miracles, Doctor. This is my niece, Rosalind. We've just met for the first time."

"I'm glad you could be here, too, Rosalind." he said, shaking her hand also. "If you'll excuse me now, I have to fill out some paperwork and make a few phone calls.

There's a snack room three doors down where you can visit privately after you've said your goodbyes here. I'll be available if you need to talk to me," he said as he turned and left the room.

"Aunt Sue," Rosalind said, "This is my boyfriend, Rusty O'Connor. We're just going to say goodbye to our friend, Bob, and we'll wait for you in the hall. Please take your time."

She reached down and touched the sheet where it covered her grandfather's hand for a brief moment of farewell. Then Rosalind and Rusty turned their attention back to Bob, whose eyes were brimming with tears.

"Could you hear any of that, Bob? Your roommate was actually Rosalind's grandfather. He carried that old pocket watch into battle. What are the chances of that? Somehow, it made it's way back across the Pacific, and into your hands, and you passed it on to Miss Leonard. It turned out to be the clue that led Rosalind to find him and her aunt. But if we hadn't been here today, we never would have known."

Bob's voice quavered as he said, "You know, he never uttered a peep the whole time we shared this room. But I'm sure gonna miss him."

Rusty took Bob's hand. "We're expected home for supper, so we're going to let you rest now. But I'll come back to see you again real soon. I promise."

Bob closed his eyes for a moment as if his soul were measuring his own days. When he opened them, he looked into Rusty's face with a telling expression.

"Don't wait too long," he said softly.

Rosalind leaned over his bedside and hugged him goodbye.

"I'll be back too," she whispered.

Out in the hall Rusty held out his arms and Rosalind walked into them, clinging to him tightly. Only he could understand how much this closure meant to her. Then he held her at arms length and asked, "Boyfriend?"

$$\sim\!\!\infty\!\!\infty\!\!\sim$$

"I'm taking Daddy home to be buried next to Mom in the Albuquerque Cemetery. Scottie was buried with his first wife in Wyoming." Sue set down her coffee cup.

Rusty leaned over and said, "Excuse me, ma'am. I'm going out to use the hall phone to call my folks and let them know we'll be a little late."

Sue nodded to him and watched as he limped away. "Rusty sure seems to be a nice young man. Have you known him long?"

"No. Not very long," Rosalind said. "Ironically, we met last July when I came down to Adrian to try to trace my mother's family."

Sue responded, "This is all so strange. Strange, and wonderful at the same time.

"Nellie was so upset when our mother divorced Dad to marry Scottie. Mom never had a chance to explain to her why she felt she had to do that. Nellie just stopped writing or answering our letters. So when we moved to Santa Fe, and then on to Albuquerque, we lost touch with her.

"We never even knew she had married, much less that she had a daughter. She seemed to want it that way. Even if she had changed her mind later on, and wanted to reach out, she didn't know where to find us." Sue breathed a sigh and paused for a moment before continuing.

"Tell me about yourself."

Rosalind took a breath and began, "My parents died when I was very little. I was raised in foster care in Phoenix until I was fourteen."

"Foster care?" Sue seemed genuinely disturbed at the idea.

"Well, I guess I should really start at the beginning. Everything I know about my past, I learned from my Grandmother Matthews who lived in Grayson, South Carolina. My father was Charles Andrew Matthews.

After World War II when he got out of the Army, he attended Grayson College. That's where he and Nellie met and fell in love. She graduated that May, and didn't know what she was going to do. She didn't know where you and your mother had gone. When my dad proposed marriage, she said yes, and they eloped.

"They lived with his parents for a little while before they found a place of their own to rent. My dad had been baptized into the LDS Church by then, but hadn't told them. When he broke the news that he was transferring to BYU, it all came out. His father was so upset that he cut them off and never spoke to my dad again."

"What about your grandmother?" Sue asked.

"My dad sent them a birth announcement when I was born. After he graduated we moved down to Florida. My Grandmother Matthews came to visit one Christmas. That was the first time she saw me, and the last time she saw Charlie and Nellie.

"It took awhile for Nellie to get over her bitterness toward your mother, so she and my dad hadn't been to the temple while they were at BYU. But once she had overcome her feelings, they drove out to be sealed in the Salt Lake Temple. Afterwards, my dad sent a postcard to

Grandmother Matthews saying we were on our way to the Grand Canyon, and would be heading home by way of South Carolina to see them.

"They were struck and killed by a drunk driver near Phoenix. I survived the wreck, and was taken to the hospital with a concussion. From there, I became a ward of the state. All I remember of my childhood was being a foster girl and shuffling from family to family."

Sue frowned. "That must have been awful for you! I feel terrible that we weren't there to help." She took another sip of coffee.

"Please don't feel bad. How could you know? Even my grandmother didn't know, really. It was unbelievably hard for her, losing her husband and son on the same day."

Sue winced at the comment. "Her husband? Your grandfather died that same day?"

"Yes. He had a heart attack. The strain must have been unbearable for her. She had a breakdown and was incapable of caring for anyone else for years. When she recovered, she immediately began a search to find me. I was fourteen years old when I was sent to South Carolina to live with her.

"We were two strangers living in the same house. I don't think she liked me very much in the beginning. I guess I was a disappointment because I wasn't at all like my dad.

"It wasn't until I had to do a family history project at school that we began to open up to each other, and then she told me all about him. But she didn't know much of anything about Nellie.

"When my parents moved out on their own, Nellie left her trunk in their attic. I found it during that history project, and began to put the pieces together as much as I could."

"What was in the trunk?" Sue asked with interest.

"There were some clothes, and a couple of Grayson College yearbooks. Mom and Dad apparently met there while they were performing in one of Shakespeare's plays. There were pictures of them as members of the cast.

"There was a travel sticker from Adrian on her trunk. So that's what led me here to try to find more information. Oh, and there were also a couple of old letters."

"Letters? From whom?"

Rosalind framed her words and answered carefully, "From you and your mother. I didn't mean to invade your privacy when I read them. I was just trying to learn all I could. I hope you understand."

"That's all right. I'm just surprised that Nellie kept them. What did they say?"

"Your letter talked about your mother and Scottie, and their plans to get married. In Bonnie's letter, she was reaching out to Nellie to try to explain her reasons for the need to declare your father dead. Scottie was moving soon, and time was running out for them," Rosalind said.

Sue sighed. "Mother and I could never understand why Nellie reacted so strongly. Daddy had been gone for so long without any news from him or the War Department, that we had given up hope."

Rusty rejoined them and took a seat next to Rosalind, and put his arm around her shoulder. She looked up at him lovingly.

"I wasn't sure what I'd find here in Adrian. Rusty and his family were so helpful when I was down here last summer. I'm just visiting for Thanksgiving, and I'll be going home to South Carolina Sunday night."

With a momentary flash of memory, Rosalind felt the same sense of dread she had had the last time she left Adrian and the O'Connors. And Rusty. She realized Sue was speaking again.

"I'm not sure how much you know of what was going on in our lives back then, so I'll just start, and you ask any questions you have.

"Mom and I, and Nellie, of course, had no idea what had happened to Daddy. The only thing we had were a couple of telegrams from the War Department. The first one said that he was missing in action. Then another came a few months later, confirming his status. It said something like 'If further information is received, the War Department will notify you.'

"We held on to hope that Daddy might still be found. After all, the telegram didn't say he had been killed, only that he was missing. But that was the last thing we ever heard.

"As time passed, Mother met Scottie, a widower, and they fell in love. I often wondered it she was just trying to escape the painful fact that she was really a widow?

"When she and Scottie decided to get married, it hadn't been a full seven years, so Daddy couldn't be declared legally dead. Mom went to see a lawyer about what legalities were involved. He told her that she deserved to go on with her life, but that to avoid any problems that might complicate things later, she really should get a divorce.

"At the time, Scottie was already preparing to move to New Mexico for a new job. So after they were married, we moved out there.

"Scottie's health never was very good. He had a heart attack when he was fifty-three, and went downhill steadily until he died in 1957.

"Mom had only a few good years of reprieve before she began to develop Alzheimer's disease. Then I became her caregiver."

In her mind, Rosalind was piecing in what her aunt had just told her with what she knew from the letters in the trunk.

"I'm sorry things were so unhappy for you, Aunt Sue," she said.

"Well, there were good times, too. I met a young man shortly after Scottie died, and we fell in love. I married outside the Church after college, and just stopped going to meetings.

"Ron, that's my husband's name, wasn't interested, and it was so hard to keep going by myself. Then I made excuses when my mom needed me around the clock.

"Toward the end, it got pretty bad. She didn't know me at all. When she became combative, I had to place her in a home. She lingered a long time.

"I had never told her about Nellie's death, because after Scottie died, she felt so guilty that she had divorced Daddy and remarried. She blamed herself for splitting the family like that.

"She hung on until last fall. She was sixty-five years old."

"What about your husband...Ron?"

"Ron and I were happy for awhile, but we divorced after about five years. Since we had no kids, I bought a double cemetery plot in Albuquerque so I could be buried beside Mom when the time came. Now I can bury Daddy there instead. I think they would both like that."

"How did you find out about your dad being here?" Rusty asked curiously.

"When Mom passed away, I submitted her obituary to the Tampa *Tribune*, because I thought there might still be people here that remembered her. Last summer, someone sent a query to the personals column of the Albuquerque paper asking for any information on a Mrs. Bonnie Scott from Adrian, Florida who had moved to New Mexico after World War II. It didn't give much information, but I realized it must have been asking about my mom. I didn't respond until a few weeks ago," she said sadly.

"Just recently, I got a call from this place asking if I were related to Wesley Martin. When I said I was, they filled me in on his medical condition, and took my name as next of kin. I wasn't sure I could handle any more drama in my life, after dealing with my mom's condition for so many years. But they said he didn't have much time left, and if I wanted to see him, I'd better come soon."

"I'm so glad you did, or we would never have met," Rosalind said taking her aunt's hands.

"Where are you staying, ma'am?" Rusty asked.

"I'm with an old friend on Orange Street. In fact, I'd better call and let her know what's going on. Then I'll call a cab." She rose stiffly.

"We can give you a lift," Rusty insisted. "Are you all finished here?"

"Yes. Everything's been taken care of. The doctor gave me a referral to a funeral home, and they'll come and pick up Daddy's body. I'll probably go back home in a few days. It still seems so strange to me. I had long since given up on ever seeing him again, just like my mom did.

"Here, let me give you my name and address," Rosalind said as she picked up a hospital note pad from the table and scribbled on it.

Sue folded it and put it into her purse. Then she took out a business card. "Here's my home address and phone number. Let's not let all of this end here."

CHAPTER EIGHT

Dusk had turned to early winter's evening, and the lights were on in the house. The O'Connors met Rusty and Rosalind at the door after they had dropped Sue off at her friend's house. They were full of questions.

"Rusty told us you found your grandfather," Evelyn said gently, putting her arm around Rosalind's waist. "Come on into the den, and let's sit for a while."

Rosalind sat down on the couch with Rusty close beside her. John and Evelyn pulled their chairs in a little closer.

"I'm still feeling a little overcome by the whole thing," she began with a catch in her throat. "I've been thinking about last summer, and being in the same room with him, without even knowing. Even then, I felt a strange connection. But I never imagined he was my grandfather." Her voice filled with emotion. "I'm still trying to get comfortable with the idea that we were a part of a miracle. Did Rusty tell you about Aunt Sue?"

"I only said that we were going to be late. I thought you might want to tell them all the details," he explained.

"After all these years of wondering about my mother's side of the family, and even then, only expecting to find some written records…" Rosalind paused.

"The way it happened was so unexpected. Aunt Sue, my mother's younger sister, was there, and we were with him when he passed away."

As the O'Connors listened, it became easier for Rosalind to share how her family search had turned out. They talked until late in the evening, stopping for sandwiches.

The unanswered question was, who had placed the query in the New Mexico newspaper? Could there be other long-lost relatives out there still to be found?

As they said goodnight, and headed to their bedrooms, Rusty caught up with Rosalind in the hall. "What would you like to do tomorrow?"

She thought a moment, and then smiled mischievously. "I think I'd like to go see Sunny Girl."

"You got it." He grinned. "But we'll have to go early. I have something else in mind for a little later."

"Sounds interesting," she said, and kissed his cheek.

He took her hand and raised it to his lips tenderly. She watched him as he limped down the hall to his room.

❧

The next morning, the two were up and about while Rusty's parents were still sleeping. They reconnoitered through the kitchen looking for something ready to eat. Rusty grabbed a few leftover rolls, and filled a thermos with some orange juice to take along with them as they headed out to Paul's place.

Their mission that morning wasn't exactly top secret. He had already filled in his dad and mom on his plans for the day, and they had whole-heartedly approved.

The Beast rolled up to the gate of Paul's ranch just as the morning sun was beginning to light up the eastern sky. There was no one in sight, so Rosalind got out of the truck, and opened the gate for Rusty to drive through. As the Beast rolled to a stop at the white rail fence surrounding the paddock, they saw Sunny Girl with her head down as she munched the lush green grass.

At the familiar sound of the truck's brakes, she looked up and whinnied. The mare looked like a beautiful statue standing there with the morning sunlight glistening on her shining red coat.

"Hey girl," Rusty called, as he offered a carrot from his pocket. She trotted over to him, and stuck her nose over the fence to sniff it, then nibbled it from his palm.

"Do you have another one?" Rosalind asked eagerly.

He gave her the last one, and when she offered it, he cautioned, "Be careful. You see what she did to me." He flexed the stubs of his fingers and laughed. After accepting the carrot, the horse allowed her to stroke her neck.

The early morning light slanted in from the east, highlighting the trees beyond the corral, and casting cool shadows here and there. There was a brisk breeze to remind them it was autumn.

As Rusty reached for Sunny Girl's halter, and rubbed the prominent blaze between her eyes, Rosalind put her arms around his waist, and held on the way she had in the Fourth of July parade, pressing her cheek against his back. He covered her arms with his and held on as long as the hug lasted.

"Let's go," Rusty said abruptly with a glint in his eye. "We're burning daylight!"

"Burning daylight?" Rosalind laughed as she released him. "Where did that come from?"

" From my favorite cowboy, John Wayne."

They climbed into the pickup and headed back to town. Rusty pulled over in front of the hardware store.

"Wait for me," he said mysteriously. "I'll be right back."

He returned a short time later with one of the store clerks in tow. They each carried big buckets of paint and bags of rollers and brushes.

Seeing the quizzical look Rosalind gave him, Rusty announced, "We're gonna paint the river house!"

"Who's *we?*"

"You, and Mom, and Dad, and me. Paul said he'd be over later on with some of his buddies to help."

Rusty's enthusiasm was contagious. "May I ask what color you've chosen?"

"Just plain old white, of course! With navy shutters, just like I wanted!"

❧ ❦

When they reached the house on the river, John and Evelyn were already there. They stood waiting beside a couple of ladders that leaned against the eaves.

"What kept you?" John asked. "We're ready to go. I'm going to do the high work."

"Thanks, Dad. You're hired," Rusty said. "I'm just glad it's not a two-story house."

"Rosalind and I can get started on the front porch," Evelyn said.

Within minutes, everyone was on task. Although no one commented on the color scheme, everyone was privately musing about what Charlene would say when she saw it.

The ladies had just about finished the porch when Paul arrived. He had brought along his brother, Herb, and their cousin, David, and his brother-in-law, Frank.

"Okay. Where do you want us, Rusty?" Paul asked as he took charge of the "late detail."

"Dad's on the ladder around back, working on the eaves. There's another ladder back there, if you want to help him with the high work, Herb. David and Frank, why don't you two pick a side of the house and get started. There's more paint and rollers and brushes in the back of my truck.

"You guys have lunch yet?" Rusty called after the four volunteers as they started off. "There's a cooler with sandwiches and the makings in the kitchen."

"Nah. We're fine," David said. "We stopped on the way over and had some burgers."

With all the help, the work went fast, and was finished by late afternoon. Everyone stood around for a few minutes, admiring the results.

"You know what would really look beautiful," Evelyn considered thoughtfully, "is some red hibiscus plants and yellow daisies under those navy shutters."

"Whatever Rusty thinks," Rosalind said knowingly with a smile." She glanced over to where the menfolk were talking.

"I owe you one, Paul. You too, Herb, Dave, Frank," Rusty said as he shook hands with each.

"Glad to help out, man. It's about time you thought of getting your own place," Paul teased.

"But you'd better work on your cooking skills," Herb said with a laugh. "Your mom's gonna be hard to replace."

"I imagine I'll still take my meals over there, at least for awhile." He grinned as the men looked over appraisingly at Rosalind.

"Thanks again, guys," Rusty said, slapping Paul on the back. "Now that you know I'm such a good painter, call me when you need some help."

ço∞ço

Driving back later to the O'Connor's house, Rusty noticed the white paint stains on Rosalind's yellow blouse.

"Looks like I owe you a shirt."

"Actually, I already have one of yours. I was bringing it back to you. If it's all the same, I'll just keep it, and we'll call it even."

Rusty looked puzzled, "One of my shirts?"

"Somehow your blue denim cowboy shirt got mixed up with my clothes the last time I was down here."

"It must have been Mom!" He laughed as he realized that his shirt had not been in Rosalind's bag by accident.

She slid over beside him, and comfortably rested her head on his shoulder. It felt so natural.

"Who would have thought my life would turn out this way? Finding my grandfather was like a miracle. And meeting Aunt Sue…

"By the way, she said she has a wedding portrait of my grandpa with my grandmother Bonnie, and a picture of him taken during the war. I asked her to make copies and send them to me. I think I'll ask for two copies of him in uniform. I'd like to give one to the museum for Miss Leonard to display with the others."

"That's a great idea," Rusty agreed. "Maybe I'll get around to taking her my photo, too."

Rosalind looked up at him and swatted his shoulder, "You mean you still haven't done that?"

"Take it easy, I've been busy doing volunteer work, caring for widows, and orphans, and such."

The moment the words came out, he wished he hadn't said them. Rosalind sat bolt upright, and the mood soured.

"I didn't mean it that way," he apologized, struggling to find the words to make it right again.

"I know you're still wondering about Charlene and me. I'd like to try to explain."

"You don't owe me an explanation," she said sadly. "I've been away a long time."

"It's not that," he said with a frown. "It started out with me going over to spend time with Russell, just trying to do what I knew Geordie would do for me and mine. But it became clear that Charlene was lonely, and needed help with things around the apartment. I guess I just missed being needed, the way you needed me."

That only made things worse.

"So you just felt sorry for me, then?" she bristled.

"No! You know that's not true! I loved you! I mean, I wanted to. But you made it pretty clear I didn't meet your expectations. I was feeling so down, that I guess I started spending time with them to fill the void."

"I see," Rosalind said sadly. "I understand."

"No! You don't!" Rusty said desperately. "Charlene wants me to be Geordie, and I can't be! And you want me to be some returned missionary, and I can't be that either!"

Rosalind thought of Hank, and as much as she hated to admit it to herself, she realized the truth in Rusty's words. She had accepted that her perception of their high school "relationship" was in the past, and would never be anything more. Maybe hanging on to just the ideal of Hank was what was holding her back.

"So where does that leave us now?" Rusty asked sarcastically. "You'll be going back Sunday night, and I'll spend the next year wondering if I'll ever see you again, just like the last time."

"Why did you ask me down here for Thanksgiving, Rusty?" Rosalind blurted out.

"I *didn't*," he almost shouted. Then, struggling to control his temper, he lowered his voice. "Mom and Dad thought if you came back, we'd be able to just pick up where we left off, and maybe, we'd find a happy ending this time.

"I know they like Charlene, and especially little Russell. But they don't think we're right for each other. They think we're both on the rebound. But she's a good woman, and I could do a lot worse..." he said bitterly. "If I can't have you."

They had driven past the O'Connor home a couple of times by now, but hadn't been ready to go in. Now he steered the Beast into the driveway, reined the truck in to a stop, and turned off the engine. They sat in silence, neither of them wanting to let go, or give in.

Finally, Rosalind spoke hesitantly. "I have two more years of college, and maybe more, if I go on for a Masters in Library Science."

"I know," he admitted dolefully, as he looked out the side window. "But I'm almost twenty-six years old now. I'd like to get married, and settle down, and have a family...with you if I could." He turned to face her.

"You know I want to marry you, Rosalind," he said with pleading eyes. "I'll give you as long as I can to decide, if you can just give me some hope."

When she didn't answer, he got out of the truck, walked around to her side, and opened her door.

The food was ready. Rusty and Rosalind did their best to be light-hearted, and recapture the mood of the afternoon for his parents' sakes. But there was an obvious change in the young couple's demeanor. After dinner, John stood up and excused himself as he left the table. "I'll be back in a minute."

Before there had been time to start another thread of conversation, he appeared at the door leading from the dining room to the den. He grinned as he held up what appeared to be a medium-sized ladies' make up case.

"It was right where I thought I'd left it. Come on."

Evelyn gave him a look of amused disbelief. "John, that's not that old record player, is it?"

"It sure is!" he said. "All the records are in the bookcase out here in the den. We're gonna have a good, old-fashioned dance party with Benny Goodman and Glenn Miller, and any of the other old-timers I can find."

John headed back into the den, and after a few minutes, and some rustling around, the upbeat sound of Kaye Kaiser's band playing a jitterbug tune filled the room.

"Well," said Evelyn. "It looks like we've been invited to a dance." She pushed the couple toward the music.

Rusty frowned skeptically. He stopped just inside the doorway, and protested. "My bum leg isn't going to let me do much dancing," he said sourly.

John looked up from sorting a stack of old 78-rpm records he had on the table. "Come on, Fred Astaire," he said to his son with a smirk. "If you can't cut a rug with Kaye Kaiser, here," he said holding up one of the records, "we'll find a slow, romantic ballad."

He removed the Kaiser platter and put on another. The lyrics of "Just the Way You Look Tonight" began to play. Rusty limped over to the couch where Rosalind had just taken a seat. He reached out to her.

"You want to dance?" he asked hesitantly.

Wanting to make an effort, Rosalind smiled and took his hand. He slowly drew her to him, breathing in the scent of her. It was a thrill to hold her in his arms as they danced cheek-to-cheek.

Rosalind closed her eyes, wanting to capture the moment. Neither of them noticed when the song finished. John winked at his wife as he put on Glenn Miller's "Moonlight Serenade."

When that one was over, he quickly put on another. It was Miller's "In The Mood" in a boogie-woogie meter.

Catching Rosalind before she could sit down, John took her hand and pulled her toward the center of the room. Unsure of the steps to such music, she began to shake her head to turn him down.

"Come on honey," he said. "It's called the Lindy. I'll teach you. There's nothing to it. I taught you to swim, didn't I?"

He tugged her arm, and she naturally did a spin. Evelyn and Rusty clapped from the couch and cheered them on.

"Just look at her, Mom," Rusty said longingly. "She just belongs in this family."

Evelyn patted her son on his good knee. "I agree. You just need to make sure she knows it before she leaves again."

"I'm trying."

CHAPTER NINE

"I'd really like to go see Miss Leonard at the museum today," Rosalind announced Saturday morning. "Do you think she'd be there on a holiday weekend?"

"Of course, dear," Evelyn answered as she took out a pan of cinnamon rolls from the oven. "It's her second home. She'll be delighted to hear all about your discoveries."

After breakfast Rusty drove her across town, and it was as though nothing had happened the day before to dampen their happiness. They sat across the desk from Miss Leonard who listened with interest as Rosalind related the incredible account of her reunion with her grandfather and long-lost aunt.

"The mystery is, who sent the query to the newspapers in New Mexico?" Rusty posed the question.

"I think I can help you with that," the retired librarian said with a slight smile. "After your visit last July, I thought about the coincidence of the pocket watch and the significance it had for you, Rosalind. I suspected that it was connected somehow to your family. It was on my mind a lot, and I became intrigued with your story. I've always loved a mystery." She laughed gently.

"I pieced together what information you had shared with me, and decided to dig a little further to see what I could find. I called Rusty's parents to ask what details you had been able to glean from the court records. John and Evelyn were kind enough to share that with me. I hope you don't mind."

Rosalind shook her head emphatically. "No. Not at all."

Satisfied, the librarian continued. "I looked up a list of the major newspapers in New Mexico. Then I wrote to place ads in the personal columns. Since I never got a response, I didn't have much hope that anything would ever come of it.

"Then, as I was reading a past issue of the Tampa *Tribune*, I came across the obituary of a Mrs. Bonnie Scott of New Mexico, naming a daughter Sue, as sole next of kin. It all seemed to fit. So I took a chance, and called the nursing home to tell them where they might be able to locate her."

"I'm so grateful to you, Miss Leonard!" Rosalind beamed through happy tears.

"Aunt Sue has a photograph of my grandfather in uniform, and she's going to send me a copy to place here in the museum. I thought I would also take a picture of the pocket watch, in case you wanted to put it in his file, or on display."

"I'd be happy to, Rosalind. It's such an important part of his story. And Rusty..." she started, but he cut her off.

"I know. I'll bring mine in Monday after work, I promise," he crossed his heart. After all she had done to help Rosalind, it was the least he could do to make her happy.

As they left the museum hand in hand, Rusty asked, "Where to next?"

"I think I'm in the mood for a cheeseburger with chili and mayonnaise."

"But we just had breakfast an hour ago!" he chided.

"I know, but there's always room for a delicious concoction like that, and a chocolate soda, of course!"

"And where would you like to eat?"

"How about on the freshly painted front porch of your future residence?" she suggested.

Rusty held the grease-soaked paper bag of sandwiches at arm's length, and opened the screen door for her as Rosalind carried the chocolate sodas up the steps. They pulled their chairs around the little table.

"You and Dad were quite a sight last night, doing the Lindy. Sorry I couldn't do the honors myself," he apologized, taking a bite out of his sandwich.

"It was fun dancing with your dad, but I preferred the slow dances," she said as she dabbed at her mouth with a paper towel.

"Yeah, they were pretty terrific." He smiled back, looking into her brown eyes and taking a long sip of his soda.

"Do you do much dancing back there?" He refrained from saying "back home."

"Only at MIA dances once in awhile."

"Oh, right, the 'Mutual in Action' thing." He deliberately misidentified it.

They attacked their sandwiches in self-defense. It was a major operation requiring their full attention to avoid spills and stains. Afterward, they licked their fingers, and settled back to relax and enjoy their sodas.

"Do you get many handsome returned missionaries as dance partners?" he asked.

"A few," she teased, "but they usually don't last too long, before some hopeful young woman captures them, or they beat it out of town to go to BYU."

"And are you one of those hopeful young women?"

Rosalind sobered a moment before answering. "Not for a while."

"And what happened to your prey," he asked with humor, but half-seriously.

"He went out to Utah to attend Brigham Young University."

"What was his name?" He brushed the crumbs off the table.

"Hank Watson. He's Emily's brother. They moved in across the street just after I came to Grayson."

Her eyes took on a faraway look as she continued. "Emily and Hank and I were like the three musketeers all through high school. Then he served a mission in California, and right after his homecoming, he left for college."

She paused to take a sip of her soda. Hopefully, that would be the end of the conversation.

"So you never saw him again?" Rusty asked without looking up.

"Well, he and Emily came home for Christmas break. That's when he told me he was going to marry someone he had met at school, a sister of a former missionary companion." She tried not to show any hint of regret. "The whole Watson family moved out to Utah before Grandmother passed away. Emily says Hank and his wife are expecting a baby next month."

"So he'll be at the wedding?" Rusty studied her closely.

"Yes. They'll be there," she said, emphasizing "they," and looked away nervously.

"Do you still love him?" He tipped his chair back against the wall, and took a noisy sip on his straw until it reached the bottom of the cup.

"Love him?" She seemed taken aback. "I never said I loved him. That was just a crush all through high school," she protested. "We never even dated. I wrote to him while he was on his mission, that's all."

"But you were disappointed when he married someone else, 'for time and all eternity'," he observed. "That must have hurt a lot."

Rosalind wondered if he were asking these questions because they deflected from his own relationship with Charlene. So she turned it back on him.

"And what about you? Charlene's been sealed to Geordie. If you married her, even if you joined the Church, it would only be a civil marriage."

"Yeah, only 'til death us do part'," he said caustically. "Just like Mom and Dad."

"You can't deny you've thought about it," she continued to dig, knowing she had struck a nerve.

"No. I can't deny it. And she's no consolation prize, either. She's wonderful, beautiful, smart, and funny…We have good times together with Russell."

He leaned forward setting the chair legs firmly on the floor. "But I know she'll always love Geordie more. I don't want to be anyone's second choice."

"And that's what you think you'd be with me?" she asked in bewilderment.

"I don't know, Rosalind. All I know is that every time I think we're really going somewhere in this relationship, you pull back. I don't know if it's the religion thing, or something else. It's like you're afraid to commit to loving me.

"I've put my feelings out there on the line. I've done everything but propose to you. But I'm just not sure you want me to!" He slammed his empty cup down on the table hard enough to produce a sharp bang.

Rosalind fell silent and looked away as she admitted to herself that he was right. She was desperately afraid if she turned him down, it would cost her everything—their friendship, their closeness.

And what about John and Evelyn? She would be giving up her place in the O'Connor family circle, and she desperately wanted that. Needed it. Without them in her life, even after finding her late grandfather and her Aunt Sue, she felt she was still just as alone as ever.

When she returned home Sunday night, it would be to an empty house, and empty dreams. Muriel was moving to North Carolina, and Mark William Dobson was...who knows where.

As she summed up what she had left, she realized it was just her coursework at Grayson College, her job, and her class of nursery children at church. Would she become one of the not-so-young women still waiting to snag a returned missionary?

She shook her head and looked up at Rusty sadly. She had no answer, and he deserved one.

"Let's change the subject," he said dismally. "Say, you've never seen the inside of this place."

He stood and pulled her out of her chair, and led her toward the double-hung front doors with their attractive, leaded glass panels. He unlocked and opened the right hand door, and stood back for her to step into the foyer.

The light that poured through the dirty windows disclosed a wonderland of golden dust particles swirling in the air. A tattered old rug barely covered the faded floorboards that had been laid down in the original structure years before.

Rusty perceived Rosalind's interest, and tried to keep the conversation going. "This is known as heart pine flooring. It's dense and heavy, insect and rot resistant, and known for its beauty, strength and durability. It will take a lot of work to restore it, but it can be done." He paused to look at Rosalind. "I guess I sound like a realtor," he said jokingly.

"I can't wait to see it when it's finished," she said, captivated.

You're the first one I want to see it, he said to himself.

"Just wait until you see the kitchen," he said, as they passed through the empty dining room. "How about this?" He proudly opened the door to a large walk-in pantry with spacious shelves reaching all the way to the ceiling.

A window above the old sink with its pump handle looked out on the overgrown backyard. The old icebox and large wood-fired cook stove had caught her attention.

She deliberated whether Rusty would insist on a restoration of the old-fashioned kitchen, or if he were open to a remodel with a newer sink, counters and appliances. She had the same daunting concern when she looked into the bathroom.

There was an old-fashioned toilet with its long flush chain hanging from the tank high above, and a large claw-footed bathtub. An oval mirror hung over a tall cabinet that held a large pitcher with a basin for a sink.

They headed back through the hall toward the front of the high-ceilinged house, passing four bedrooms. The front one had a long row of built-in bookshelves.

"This might have been used as a den or office at one time," he said.

In the parlor, a large fireplace with a beautifully carved mantle dominated the room. She could picture a warm, crackling fire going with little stockings hanging there, and a large Christmas tree in the front window.

"It's all yours, if you want it." Rusty interrupted her thoughts as he stepped closer. "But it's a package deal. This broken-down Marine comes with it, along with a couple of meddling, middle-aged in-laws living close by.

"There are no guarantees, Rosalind, but I think I could make you happy. I know I'd spend my life trying."

"But what about my finishing college?" Rosalind said with an uneasy frown.

There was her barrier going up again. Still, he saw an opening, and feeling a little more hopeful than before, he took it.

"We have colleges and universities all over Florida." He lifted her chin and smiled indulgently. "I'm sure you could find one you liked within driving distance of Adrian in that blue Malibu of yours." He pronounced it with a French accent like *bloo molly boo*.

"Unless, of course, you wanted to start a family right away," he grinned. "Then you could take your time about graduating. I know a pair of great babysitters who would love to spoil rotten any grandchildren who might come along.

"Speaking of which, just to sweeten the deal, I don't know if you noticed it or not, but Sunny Girl didn't put on that extra weight just eating carrots. She's dropping a foal in the spring. Paul says I can have first dibs on it."

"That would make an interesting engagement ring." Rosalind giggled.

"Does that mean you accept?" Rusty asked, only partly joking.

Rosalind looked seriously into his blue eyes. "Will you let me have until the end of the spring semester to give you my answer? That's only six months. I'll have my first two years of college by then, in case I need to transfer, I mean." She thought it sounded like a reasonable request.

"And will you be able to transfer your affections by then, too?" he asked earnestly.

A flash of uncertainty flickered in her eyes for just a moment, but she spoke firmly. "You'll have my answer by then, no later."

"All right. That's not so long to wait, I guess. I'll be here. May I kiss you, Rosalind?"

She reached her arms around about his neck and moved closer. He had no hesitancy in holding her in his arms. His kiss was powerful but not demanding. There was that thrill again, the attraction she had only felt for him.

Is this what it's like to really love someone?

As they drove the miles back to the O'Connor home, Rusty kept silent as he held her hand. He believed he had made it as clear as he could. He had agreed to wait, but there was a deadline. He knew he had to prepare mentally for the chance that her answer would be no. And he had no reason to believe that it wouldn't be.

CHAPTER TEN

As Rusty and Rosalind prepared to leave for church early Sunday morning, John pulled him aside conspiratorially. "Do you think it might help if your mom and I drove you over in our car? That way, if the subject came up, you wouldn't have to invite *anyone* else to come spend the afternoon with you. We could even stay for church, and kind of run interference for you."

Seeing the concerned look on his dad's face, Rusty considered his serious offer. Trying not to chuckle, he shook his head negatively.

"I think I can handle it, Dad. But thanks anyway." He was amused at the whole idea, and wondered if his father had heard about polygamy in the early years of the Mormon Church.

Evelyn was waiting at the front door to tell them goodbye. "Now try not to be too late," she urged with concern.

"We'll do our best, Mom," Rusty smiled and kissed his mother's cheek.

❧❧

"Hello, Bro. O'Connor. It's good to see you again," said the man at the chapel door.

Rosalind was surprised that the greeter remembered Rusty's name. Then she saw Charlene waving from the left side of the chapel where she was holding seats for them. It was obvious, he had attended the ward before with her and her boy.

Russell stood up in the pew and called out none too softly, "There he is, Mama. There's our Rusty!"

They crossed the chapel to join them. Russell pulled Rusty into a space between him and his mother, leaving Rosalind to sit on the aisle, feeling more than a little bit uncomfortable.

A man leaned over her to whisper something to Rusty. He nodded, excused himself, and rose to leave. "I'll be back in a little bit," he said.

Rosalind watched him as he walked over to where the deacons sat facing the Sacrament Table, and took a seat with them. Incredulous, she turned to Charlene who proudly announced in a whisper, "Rusty took the missionary discussions at our place. He was baptized in August. He struggled with doubts at first, but we finally won him over, didn't we Russell? He's been ordained a Priest in the Aaronic Priesthood."

"Yeah. We told him all about the Joseph Smith story and the Book of Mormon, and how the Gospel was restored. And now he's a member of the Church, just like my daddy." Russell beamed as he spoke.

"And I've been workin' on John and Evelyn, too," Charlene said confidently. "Last month I brought her out to a Relief Society work meetin'. She seemed to really enjoy it. Convincin' John's gonna be harder, but I think if I can get Evelyn baptized, he'll come along sooner or later. That will make Rusty happier. I know he worries about what's gonna happen when he tells them he became a Mormon."

Rosalind was having a hard time absorbing all this news. In the first place, she was very uncomfortable with the way Charlene spoke so casually about "converting John and Evelyn." In the second place, why hadn't Rusty told her he'd been baptized?

Then it occurred to her that, maybe it was because Charlene and Russell had been able to convince him to investigate the Church, while she herself had never even discussed conversion with him. She felt like such a failure.

The look on Charlene's face was one of complete triumph during the ordinance of the Sacrament, as she accepted the bread, and then the water, from the trays Rusty offered. He reverently avoided making eye contact with either woman, but did manage a brief smile at Russell who watched him with utter hero worship.

Once the ordinance was completed, Rusty returned to his seat again, struggling to stay neutral. Russell eased the situation by climbing up onto his lap. But then Charlene put her arm around *her* man's shoulder.

The situation was almost unbearable for Rosalind, and yet somehow, comical. Knowing the feelings he had shared with her, she really felt sorry for him, being trapped in this triangle.

What will happen if I turn him down, and he ends up marrying this woman? Could he ever really be happy with her?

Luckily, Charlene had been unable to get a substitute teacher, so she left to teach her class after opening exercises. Rusty walked young Russell to Junior Sunday

School. Then he and Rosalind attended the Gospel Doctrine class.

When the Sunday school class came to order, the teacher, Brother Black, asked if there were any visitors present. Rusty stood and introduced Rosalind as a friend of the family, so there would be no gossip getting back to Charlene. At the end of class, an elderly woman in a wheelchair approached Rosalind, and reached out her frail hand.

"I'm Sister Lockhart. I knew your grandmother, Bonnie," she said. "I lived next door, and sometimes I watched Nellie and Susie for her when they were little."

Rosalind took the wrinkled, age-spotted hand in hers. "It's so great to meet you, Sister Lockhart. You're the first person I've met who knew my mother."

The old lady was happy to feel useful, and wanted to do more to help. "I think I may still have a picture of them playing out in my yard. I don't know why I kept it all these years, except it was a pretty good picture of me in the background. I was a real looker back then," she winked and said mischievously.

Rosalind laughed and squeezed her hand softly.

"If I can find it, I'll bring it to Charlene so she can mail it to you."

"Thank you so much, Sister Lockhart. That would be wonderful!" Rosalind leaned down to give the elderly woman a gentle hug.

She looked about for Rusty to share the news. But he was already down the hall at the door of Russell's classroom. Charlene found him first, and the three of them came down the hall toward the foyer, she with her arm linked through his.

Rosalind ducked around the corner. She took a seat on the couch in the foyer beside a harried young woman wrestling an infant and a rowdy toddler. With a questioning smile at the mother, she offered her arms to the child who went to her willingly. The little girl was content to sit on her lap until the others joined her. Rusty was bemused at the scene, but Rosalind just smiled sweetly.

"I get a lot of experience in the nursery," she explained, as she continued a game of patty cake with the child.

"I have to go now," she said to the little girl. "Are you ready to go back to your mommy?" The now calmer child shook her head, and climbed off Rosalind's lap.

On their way out to the parking lot, Charlene was still attached to Rusty's arm. "Don't forget, Sweetie. You're coming over for a visit just as soon as you can."

They had reached the pickup truck. She and Russell hugged Rusty one more time. Then she turned and said sweetly, "I hope you have a good flight home, Rosalind. Come back and see us real soon." She leaned her head on Rusty's shoulder as she spoke.

"Thanks. I hope I will," Rosalind replied, waving goodbye to Russell.

As Rusty helped Rosalind up to the seat of the truck, Charlene called after him, "Sweetie, did you ever find my lipstick? I think I left it in the glove box."

Rusty stiffened, and tossed an answer over his shoulder. "No. But I'll be sure to get it back to you, if it turns up."

They drove several miles down the road in silence before Rosalind was able to steal a glance at him. He wore a stern, uncomfortable look that made her giggle at his predicament.

He relaxed a little, and chuckled, too. "Who knew I would turn out to be such a fine catch? Imagine, two women scratching it out over me!"

"Scratching it out?" Rosalind pretended offense. "I'm not scratching it out with anyone!"

Now he laughed more loudly.

"But, I do have to ask, Rusty. Why didn't you tell me you had joined the Church?" There was a hint of hurt in her voice.

"I guess I was afraid to. I mean, not afraid exactly…but what if it didn't 'take'? What if I couldn't stay with it? It's a very demanding religion, you know. It's not like just going to church occasionally when you feel like it, even if it's only at Christmas, or Easter, or Mother's Day. I guess I was sort of giving it a 'test drive' or something."

"You mean you didn't really have a testimony when you were baptized?" Rosalind asked with alarm.

"I don't know. I thought I did. But I got all caught up in trying to please Russell, and Charlene too, I guess."

Worried where this was leading, he glanced over at her helplessly.

"I want you to know that I didn't do it for you, Rosalind. That day you left me at the bus station, I was so angry that I was ready to give up on everything!" His hands tightened on the steering wheel at the memory.

"I found one last cigarette under the seat, and reached for my spare lighter in the glove box. But it was stuck, and I couldn't get into it. That made me even angrier, so I beat on it with my fist, and it finally popped open. It had jammed on the *Book of Mormon* Russell gave me that night. I must have stuffed it in there when we were leaving the parking lot.

"I took it out, and instead of smoking, I started reading. Then I couldn't stop. I kept it under the seat of the truck. Sometimes I would take it with me out to the river house and sit on the porch and read. I even tried to imagine us sitting there, reading it together." He smiled slightly at the memory, and then continued.

"I took the missionary lessons at Charlene's because I

didn't want Mom and Dad to know. I didn't want them to think I was doing it just to get you to marry me. But instead, Charlene got so wrapped up in all of it, that she thought I was doing it for her and Russell. That's what he thought, too. When the missionaries gave me the challenge, I looked at his hopeful, little face, and I just couldn't let him down. So I said yes. And that's all there was to it."

"So you were only baptized out a sense of duty then?" she asked with disappointment.

"Yeah. No!" He looked out the window in frustration. "I mean, I guess so."

"You haven't answered the real question, Rusty. Do you believe the Gospel is true?" Rosalind asked with tears in her eyes.

"If it meant I could spend all eternity with you, I'd believe it in a minute. But how can it mean that much to me in my life, if the most I can hope for, is being a substitute Dad and husband?"

"There are other LDS women out there. You might still find someone else." She looked at him directly. "But don't you see, you can't do it for me, or for Charlene, or even for little Russell. You have to get your own testimony. You have to ask Heavenly Father for yourself if the Church is true. You can't live on borrowed light."

Her tears flowed down her cheeks. "I can't help you with that, Rusty, not now, not next spring, not ever. You have to find that out for yourself."

●●●

Lunch with the O'Connors was delicious, as usual. The mood was light, and the conversation, playful.

"So when did you say you're coming back down here,

young lady," John asked bluntly.

"Not until after classes are over next semester," she answered and glanced at Rusty.

"Well, you know you're welcome here any time, honey," Evelyn patted her hand lovingly.

As Rosalind was finishing up her packing, Evelyn came into the room.

"He loves you, you know."

"I know he does," Rosalind responded. "And I love him. But there are complications."

"Do you mean because of Charlene?"

Rosalind smiled slightly, and shook her head.

"Is there someone else?" Evelyn asked.

"No. Not really. Maybe just an ideal of someone. It's hard to explain."

"He's a really good man, Rosalind. You'll find none better. He's honest, and loyal, and he'll make a really good father. I know he'd take good care of you. And unless you tell him not to, he'll wait for you until hell freezes over." Her voice cracked when she spoke the last words.

Rosalind reached out and hugged her, knowing she was right. He would wait, until she told him not to. Her heart was heavy.

Perhaps Evelyn was pleading with her to make a decision now, and not prolong her son's pain. But every time she was on the verge of saying yes, something inside told her no.

Still, things had changed this time. Maybe she was the one who was waiting now. Waiting to see the outcome of Rusty's struggle for certainty over the Church. The ball was in his court, she realized. But she couldn't expect Evelyn to understand any of this.

After the farewell ritual, Rosalind and Rusty climbed into the Beast, and once more drove the familiar road to Tampa. This time they turned off toward the airport.

"You'll write to me, won't you Rusty?" she asked.

"You mean, like you wrote to me?" he joked.

"You know what I mean. You'll let me know how you're feeling?"

"You mean whether an angel came down and zapped me with a finger, and told me it was all true?" He laughed without humor.

Rosalind struggled to make her point. "No. I mean how you're getting along, and whether your feelings change about the Church, or me, or Charlene."

"I promise. I won't marry anyone else, without letting you know. You get first dibs," he grinned. "And what about you? Are you going to give serious thought to my proposal? I need to let Paul know about your engagement gift."

"I think you should definitely buy the foal!" She laughed. "And you know I will, Rusty. I'll think about it all the time. You and your parents are all I've got now."

"Hey! You'd be marrying me, not my family!"

"I know it, silly. But it is nice to be welcomed by your folks the way they've welcomed me. It feels like they actually love me."

"They do! And if you end up walking away, they'll never let me live it down that I disappointed them!"

"Oh, Rusty, you really know how to put the pressure on!" she laughed.

"That's what we Marines are known for, ma'am. When we have an objective, we don't give up easily." He reached over and pulled her beside him.

"Well, just don't give up on me yet, Rusty. Give me time. And by the way, you're a civilian now."

"'Once a Marine, always a Marine.'" He grinned. "I said I'd wait, didn't I? But I don't have to like it." The grin turned into a good-natured frown.

"All I'm asking you to do, is just go the distance. Get your answer."

∽৵৶

Rusty pulled the truck up to the curb at the departure area of the airport where passengers could access the airline ticket counters to finalize their flights. The occupants of several other vehicles were hastily saying their goodbyes.

"There's usually a big traffic jam. This will get you to the ticket counter a lot quicker."

He turned and gave her a quick kiss on the cheek. "I'm going to miss you, Rosalind," he said, "and so will Mom and Dad."

"I'll miss you too, Rusty. Okay. Then I guess it's goodbye for now," she said nervously, feeling hurried by the other drivers.

As she reached for the door handle, Rusty put his hand lightly on her shoulder. "Stay here," he said. "I'll go around and get your bags."

Rusty lifted them out of the bed of the truck and set them on the concrete next to the Beast. He opened her door, and helped her out of her seat. When she started to reach down for them, he said, "Hold it. I'll carry them inside for you." He took a bag in each hand and followed her to the entrance, and set them down again just inside the door.

"Well, I guess this is as far as I go. I need to move the truck out of temporary parking before I get a ticket."

"This is fine," she said. "I can take it from here." She looked up into his blue eyes. "Thanks for everything, Rusty."

He gently pulled her to him for a brief kiss, then let her go. Suddenly, a strong emotion overwhelmed him, almost bringing him to tears. Putting his arms around her, he kissed her as though it were for the last time.

"I'm not going to say goodbye, Rosalind. What's been growing inside you and me is not going to end here," he said with determination.

"Then, so long for now, Rusty." She turned away and began to walk to the Eastern Airline desk.

He watched her for a few moments, then hurried back toward the curb where his truck, engine still running, waited for him. An impatient driver honked his horn at him, but Rusty just smiled and waved as he climbed behind the wheel.

Rosalind stopped a few feet from their parting. She didn't have a clear notion of what she would do. In a fraction of a second, she knew she would just turn and smile. But Rusty was gone. Disappointed, she continued on toward the airline counter.

As Rusty drove away from the curb, a devastating cloud of despair descended upon him. He recognized it at once, and knew all too well the dangerous paths where this dark mood could lead him.

He turned off into the parking lot where he pulled into a space to sit and think. He felt sick. Maybe he should go home.

His hands were shaking now. Sweat beaded his brow. The dreaded panic had returned.

As in the past, he was trapped, unable to move, cut off,

and unable to get back to safety. The attack was almost suffocating.

He grabbed the steering wheel, and hung on as tremors racked his whole body. It hadn't been this bad in a long time.

In desperation, he prayed for deliverance from the anguish and desolation that enveloped him, and kept him bound. Then he closed his prayer, and waited.

Gradually, he began to feel relief from his suffering. His clinched hands let go of the wheel, and he flexed them to restore circulation. Recalling counseling sessions and the coping mechanisms he had been taught in the VA hospital, he analyzed what was going on to trigger such a relapse of his battle fatigue.

Reviewing his life, he acknowledged that he had a strong support system in his caring parents who were always there for him. Workwise, he had a good job he enjoyed, that gave him the chance to contribute, and to have a sense of fulfillment. As for his survivor's guilt, he had built a relationship with Geordie's widow, Charlene, and his boy, Russell, that allowed him to honor the memory of his childhood friend. At the thought of them, his tension returned, and began to rise.

Then he pictured the face of that sweet brown-eyed, brown-haired South Carolina girl, who had so captivated him. He recognized that the two strongest motivations in his life were his love for Rosalind Matthews, and the struggle to attain what she was expecting of him.

He knew she was right about his having to know for himself about the Gospel. In his heart, he knew it was true. Why couldn't he just admit it to himself? He had to be able to tell her that he knew.

He looked at his watch, and had a strong feeling that he should not go home right now. Instead, he wanted to go to the Tampa Ward Sacrament Meeting. There was still time to make it even though he might be a little late.

Pondering this impulse to go to church, he realized it had nothing to do with Rosalind, or Charlene, or even her boy. He just wanted to be there.

He glanced in the mirror, and wiped his face with his handkerchief. A few deep breaths, and he was ready. He cranked the engine, pulled out of the parking lot, and headed back toward the LDS Chapel.

CHAPTER ELEVEN

It was so late when Rosalind arrived home that night, that she stretched out on the living room couch, telling herself she would just rest a few minutes. But sleep quickly overcame her.

At seven o'clock the next morning, the ringing of the telephone awakened her. She stumbled toward the hall, checking her watch as she went. When she realized how long she had overslept, she was shocked fully awake, as if cold water had been thrown in her face. She had a class at nine o'clock.

Wondering who would be calling so early, Rosalind picked up the receiver. "Hello," she said.

"Roz? I've been trying to reach you all weekend. Where were you?" She recognized Emily Watson's unmistakable voice from the other end.

"I went to visit friends for Thanksgiving. What's the matter, Emily? What's wrong?"

"Hank's baby came early, on Friday. And Crystal didn't make it. It's so terrible," she sobbed.

"Crystal's dead?" Rosalind reacted numbly, as she tried to respond.

"Yes. She died in childbirth."

Trying to gather her wits, she asked, "What about the baby? How's the baby?"

"It's a little girl. She's tiny, but she's holding her own. She's still in the hospital. Poor Hank! He's so overcome with grief, that he doesn't know what to do from one minute to the next. The doctor had to order him out of the room, so they could do what they needed to do." Emily paused to blow her nose.

"Dad and his bishop are trying to help him make all the arrangements for the funeral and everything. They called Crystal's parents because Hank was in no shape to do it."

"Emily, do they know what happened? Why did they lose her?"

"She had toxemia. I guess they call it 'preeclampsia' now. That's high blood pressure, and protein in the urine. She had been having swelling, and sudden weight gain, and headaches in the past few weeks. It progressed, and she started having seizures during delivery. Then she went into a coma. The doctors did all they could. But it happened so fast, and then she was gone."

For a moment, Emily's voice broke down, and she was unable to form a coherent word. She struggled to regain her composure.

"Oh Roz, it's so sad. Hank is alone now to raise his little daughter."

"Emily, I'm so sorry! I wish there were something I could say or do to help. Are you still going forward with your wedding next month?"

"We have to. Hank was supposed to be best man though, and I don't know if he'll be up to it. I guess it might be good to give him something else to occupy his mind, though.

"Rosalind," she said using her formal name, "the Gospel is supposed to help us get through things like this, but it doesn't take away the pain right now. Dad gave him a Priesthood blessing last night. The baby's supposed to be released to go home Tuesday, if all goes well. I just hope Hank will be ready.

Thinking ahead, Emily said, "I know Mom and Dad will do all they can to help, so he can get through this next semester. He may have to give up his apartment, and move back home with them. But he shouldn't make any serious decisions like that until he can think it through.

"Well, I knew you would want to know. And I just really needed to talk to my best friend," Emily sniffed.

"Call me anytime you need to, Emily. I'll be out there in a few weeks. Please give all your family my love. And please let Hank know how very sorry I am. He and the baby will be in my prayers."

Rosalind struggled to pay attention in her English Literature class. The professor's delivery was dry at best, and her thoughts kept returning to Emily's call. It was so hard to accept. Her thoughts ran ahead unbidden.

Crystal was there with Hank, just at the happiest day of their life together, the birth of their child. And then she was gone. Did she even get to see her baby? Did she get to hold her? Probably not. Did the baby have a name yet?

She made it home after work that evening without falling asleep at the wheel. After a light supper, she went to bed early, making sure to set the clock this time.

She awoke the next morning before the alarm went off. Then she knelt beside her bed to say her morning prayers.

She gave thanks for all the many blessings she had received, especially for having seen her grandfather before his passing, and meeting her Aunt Sue. She expressed her thanks for Rusty and his family, and prayed fervently that he would find answers to his questions. She prayed for a blessing of peace, and comfort, and healing for Hank, and for him to find the strength to get through this time in his life, and to be able to take care of his baby girl.

A hot shower rejuvenated her. She dressed and headed for the kitchen. Though she wasn't hungry, she knew she had to keep up her strength. So she scrambled herself a couple of eggs, made toast, and had a glass of orange juice. With time to spare, she drove down to the college, and found a good parking space so she wouldn't have far to walk to class.

❧

That night, she wrote a note thanking John and Evelyn for their hospitality. Then she wrote a separate note to Rusty. She didn't mention Hank, or the tragedy that had struck his little family. She tried to sound upbeat, and affectionate, and to say all the things she thought he would like to hear. She signed it, "Love, Rosalind."

Then she took out a sympathy card from an assortment in her desk drawer, and wrote a note to Hank at the Watson's address. Without even thinking, she signed it "Love always, Rosalind."

She studied what she had written, and especially the closing and signature. She worried whether or not she should send it that way. Was it appropriate? But in the end, she sealed it and put it with the other two to mail the next day.

There are different shades of love, she thought, admitting to herself that he was her first love. As such, he would always hold a special place in her heart.

Rosalind leaned forward and put her head in her hands. She felt a twinge of guilt as the thought of Crystal crossed her mind. Understandably, she had been more concerned about Hank and the Watson family.

Now Crystal, a girl she had never met, began to weigh heavily on her mind. *What kind of person was she? Would we have been friends?*

She must have been pretty wonderful if Hank loved her so much. She was starting what should have been the most wonderful and glorious part of her life, as a young mother with a loving husband.

How sad. What is Heavenly Father's purpose in such unhappiness? Do I really believe that everything has a purpose? Oh, Crystal! Poor Crystal.

Tears began to fall. She cried herself to sleep, sitting at the desk with her head resting on her arms.

৩৽৵

"Hi, Roz."

Rosalind looked up at the young woman standing before her. "You're Crystal," she said. "Isn't this strange? We've never met, yet I know you."

"Yes. I am Crystal. And it's not as strange as you think. You and I have been friends for a long time."

"I'm glad you came," said Rosalind, not needing to ask from where she had come.

"Thank you for caring about me, Roz. I just want you to know that I'm all right. Will you help Hank to know that? I can't seem to get through to him."

"I'm glad to know you're well. I will tell Hank," Rosalind said, expecting her to melt away. But Crystal continued to stand before her, and smiled so wistfully that Rosalind felt certain she was on another mission as well.

"There's something else, isn't there?" she asked.

"Yes," Crystal said, still smiling. "You need to know that you have your whole life ahead of you. You're free to make decisions. You can fulfill the measure of your creation, Roz."

"What does that mean, 'the measure of my creation?'"

"You know. Ask Heavenly Father to bless your life. I'll be watching. See ya' later, Roz. Kiss my baby for me."

✐

Rosalind awoke with a pain in her neck, and sat up straight in her chair. The sky just outside her window was beginning to turn light gray as dawn was breaking. Looking around the room, she realized that she had spent the night at her desk.

What was it? She asked herself. *It was just a dream*, she rationalized.

If it were a dream, it was very real. She struggled to get it back piece by piece.

She had had a perfect image of Hank's wife, Crystal. They had talked as friends. She had had a deep and loving feeling for this girl in her dream, or was it a vision?

Two things came to mind, and she knew that she must accomplish them. It was as if she had received a personal revelation. She would be a comfort to Hank. And she would take hold of the happiness that lay within her own reach.

Yes, everything has a purpose. All my unhappy years, my grandmother, my parents...

She knew too that her trip to Adrian, and meeting Rusty and the O'Connors, had happened for a reason. She thought of him and the struggle he was going through to find his testimony for himself.

As she pondered, a strong feeling washed over her. *Rusty will be all right.* Her heart was at peace.

With the trip to Utah ahead of her, and helping Emily and Hank, she had a lot to work through. Thoughts of Crystal came back to her mind.

What was it she had said? "You can fulfill the measure of your creation?"

She showered and dressed, and went downstairs to have some breakfast. As she finished her toast, she realized that she felt much more positive today, as a clarity of thought came over her.

She was aware of all the pain and chaos around her, but she knew with certainty that Heavenly Father was in control. Everything would work out in His own time. With that, she reached for the phone book, and made a call to book airline reservations to Utah.

CHAPTER TWELVE

The days had passed quickly, and as her plane touched down at the Salt Lake City airport on a Thursday afternoon, a carpet of snow covered the ground. It was bitterly cold, and she pulled her red plaid, wool scarf tightly about her neck as she made her way down the aircraft's steps to the tarmac.

Passengers streamed into the terminal. Once inside, Rosalind stepped aside of the rush, and stopped to get her bearings. She looked for familiar faces in the crowd waiting to welcome someone from the incoming flight.

A familiar voice called out over the noise, "Rosalind! We're over here."

There stood her very own welcoming committee: Brother and Sister Watson and some of the younger Watson children. Rosalind waved and hurried over to meet them.

Patricia Watson stepped forward and gave her a big welcoming hug. "We're so glad you're here. How was your flight?" she asked.

Before she could answer, Phil Watson enveloped her in one of his famous bear hugs. It reminded her of Rusty's dad. "Welcome to Utah," he said.

"It's good to be here, " Rosalind said. "But it's so cold! I feel like a popsicle."

Phil laughed. "Few places are colder than Utah in the winter," he said. "Antarctica to name one. Give me your claim check and I'll go pick up your luggage. I'll meet you all downstairs at the main exit."

Three of the Watson children who had come along enveloped her in a group hug. "Look at you kids," she said. "You're practically grown up."

She looked up at their mother. "I don't see Carrie. I guess she didn't come?"

"She's at home watching her new little niece. Emily is at a fitting session for her wedding dress, and Hank is…busy. So they couldn't come with us."

Phil had already picked up Rosalind's luggage and was waiting at the exit when they got there. "Listen, everybody. You all wait here where it's warm. I'll go get the car, and pull around to pick you up at the curb. We need to hurry home before the storm hits. The weatherman is predicting a lot more snow."

Within a few minutes, they were all in the car. The heater was beginning to warm up the inside.

"Emily sends her love," Pat said. "She's lost some weight in the past few weeks. The seamstress has to take up her wedding dress a little in the waist. We'll see her at home later."

"I was so sorry to hear about Crystal. How is Hank doing?" Rosalind asked.

"He's still struggling," Pat said, turning to speak over the front seat. "He's missed a lot of classes. We're just hoping he can make it through the semester.

"He's talking about dropping out for a year or two to get his bearings. Of course, we've tried to advise him against that. He would lose his scholarship if he did, and he might never go back to college.

"He only has a part-time job. He would have to find something full-time with benefits and insurance."

"How is the baby?" Rosalind asked.

"She's beautiful! So tiny and perfect. He named her Emily Rose, and plans to call her Rose. She looks just like Hank at that age, doesn't she, Phil?"

Emily Rose. It's a beautiful name.

৩৯৩৯

They hurried into the Watson house just as the snow began to come down heavily. Carrie tiptoed out of the kitchen, shushing everyone. She pointed to the bassinet in the corner.

"I finally got her back to sleep. She wants to eat every couple of hours, but she doesn't take much formula at a time."

"Hello, Carrie." Rosalind reached out to give her a warm hug.

The lanky teenager looked so different. Her bangs had grown out and her long blond hair was pulled back into a ponytail. The new look suited her.

"I'm so glad you came, Rosalind. It's so great to see you again!" she said sincerely.

Phil and Brian collected the winter coats, hats and scarves. They took them out to the mudroom off the garage to hang them up.

"I'll make us some hot chocolate," Pat said as she went to the kitchen.

From the bassinet in the corner came a whimpering sound. Carrie leaned over to check on her little charge.

"Well, that was a short nap, wasn't it, missy? Oh, you need a change, huh?" She pulled a tiny newborn-sized disposable diaper from an opened package of Kimbees beside the rocker. After the diapering was done, Carrie was about to put Rose back into the bassinet.

"May I hold her?" Rosalind reached out.

"Sure, here you go." Carrie relinquished the baby into her arms.

Wide eyes looked up at Rosalind in wonder. Tiny fists waved in the air. She was so small and delicate. The sleeves of her newborn "onesie" were rolled up several times. Her thin legs nearly came out of it as she drew them up to her tummy, and then kicked them out again.

Rosalind tried to adjust the garment, but gave up and wrapped her securely in a pink baby shawl Carrie offered. She sat down in the rocking chair beside the fireplace.

"Hello, Baby," she cooed. "Hello, little Rose."

"Here, you might need this," Carrie cautioned. She draped a cloth diaper over Rosalind's shoulder for a burp pad.

Rosalind lifted the infant to an upright position against her shoulder. The tiny, bobbing head brushed her cheek. Rose's warm, moist breath felt so good on her skin. Patting her back lightly came naturally. *It must be instinct*, she thought.

The stamping of feet on the door mat on the front porch announced Hank's arrival. As he opened the storm door and stepped inside, Rosalind gaped at him. He had changed so drastically that she barely recognized him.

When he took off his coat and muffler, she could see how thin he was, almost gaunt. His red-rimmed eyes reflected the pain he had felt over the last couple of weeks.

He looked through those in the living room as though he hadn't seen them, and walked straight back to the kitchen to find his parents.

"It's there," he announced with resignation. "They placed the gravestone today before the storm hit. So that's taken care of."

Phil and Patricia hugged their son tightly.

"Rosalind's here, did you see her?" Phil asked, patting him on the back.

"No. I didn't even notice. I guess I should go say hello."

He approached the back of the rocking chair quietly. The tiny face of his infant daughter peeked over Rosalind's shoulder.

"Hello, Roz. How are you?"

She turned her head slightly to look up at him. "I'm fine, Hank. You have a beautiful daughter. What a blessing."

"Yeah. She is beautiful. I just wish Crystal could have seen her. She would be so proud."

His eyes brimmed with tears. He wiped them away, and reached out to rub the baby's back tenderly.

"Oh, I guess you want to hold her," Rosalind offered.

"No. You go ahead. She seems pretty contented there. She usually cries when I hold her." He smiled weakly and ran his fingers through his tousled hair.

"You're just getting to know each other," Rosalind reassured him. She kissed Rose on her soft, blond hair, and enjoyed her baby scent.

"I think she likes women better," he laughed softly. "With her aunts and her grandmother taking care of her when I'm at work and class, she hasn't had much time to 'bond' with me, or whatever they call it."

Rose's eyelids were fluttering. Soon she was dozing on Rosalind's shoulder.

"I was sorry to hear about your losing your grandmother last Easter," Hank said. How is everything going in Grayson? Are you doing okay?"

"Yes. I'm still working part-time at the college library and carrying a full load of classes. I bought a car, a blue, 1969 Chevelle Malibu," she said with a sense of pride.

"Mrs. Dobson is thinking of moving to North Carolina to live with her daughter and son-in-law. Mark William went through a bad time, and left home for a while. He came back for Grandmother's funeral, though. And he and his mother seemed to work things out. He's gone again now, though, and I don't know if she will hold on to the house for him or sell it. If she doesn't sell, she'll have to rent it out to someone."

Hank's only response was an occasional, "Oh."

"I've made a couple of trips down to Adrian, Florida to search for my mother's family, and the most wonderful things have happened. I searched at the county courthouse in Tampa last summer, and I found the marriage license and certificate of my grandparents, Wesley Martin and Bonnie Hudson. I also found a deed for a house they bought. But it wasn't there when I looked for it. It must have burned down.

"I did find the birth certificates of my mother and her sister Sue. The hardest part was finding the divorce record for my grandparents, Bonnie and Wesley, and her second marriage to a Mr. Scott."

Rosalind realized she was talking more than was necessary, but she was carrying on a one-way conversation, and couldn't help it. Hank did seem to relax a little in his chair, so she just kept talking.

"There's a retired librarian in Adrian who is gathering memorabilia for an historical museum. Someone had donated a pocket watch that played 'My Bonnie Lies Over the Ocean.' On the back of the case, it was engraved with 'Together Forever.'

"When I went down there again at Thanksgiving, I miraculously located my grandfather in a nursing home. I got to see him just before he died. My mother's sister, Sue, was there, too. Here's the amazing part. That old pocket watch was his. He had carried it to war with him in the Pacific, and just before going into battle, he gave it to someone to bring back, if he didn't make it."

Grateful not to have to talk, Hank acknowledged what she was saying, and nodded occasionally. He seemed to make a genuine effort to follow the conversation. But he was very tired.

She realized she was giving him more information than he could comprehend. She should wait, and share any more of her discoveries with Emily.

The phone rang, and Pat picked up the kitchen extension. "Hi Emily. Oh, I'm glad she was able to fix it. All right. Be careful driving. We'll hold dinner until you get here."

She hung up the receiver and turned to her son. "Hank, Emily is on her way, so you have time to lie down for a nap if you'd like."

"Thanks, Mom. I think I will." He rose slowly, and as an afterthought he asked, "Will you be okay with the baby, Roz?"

"Oh, sure. I'm enjoying her." She smiled up at him with contentment.

"You look like a natural. Thanks." He turned away with a tired smile.

Hank had slept right through dinner. Phil carried the bassinet into their bedroom so the baby wouldn't disturb him if she woke up.

Emily and Rosalind picked up as if they had never been apart. They spent the meal finishing each other's sentences, as good friends often do.

Pat found a rare pause in their conversation. "Rosalind, we're putting you in with Emily in her room for the night. That way, you two can visit and catch up after dinner."

"That's perfect, Mom," Emily said.

Everyone else had finished their dinner, and wandered away from the table. "Well, I'll get this all cleared up," Pat said as she began stacking plates.

"Let us do that, Sister Watson. We can do the dishes, too," Rosalind offered. "You have your hands full." Then just as they used to, she asked her friend, "Do you want to wash or dry?"

When they had finished their self-appointed chore, the girls told the family goodnight, and retreated to Emily's room. They stayed up and talked and laughed quietly, long after everyone else had gone to bed.

Rosalind shared the joy while her friend chattered on excitedly about how handsome and wonderful her fiancé, Brad, was. She talked of all the plans they had for the future. It was almost like old times, sharing the most important things in their lives.

The conversation soon turned to the wedding. "Your outfit is hanging in the closet, Roz. Try it on."

Emily pulled out the tea-length, full-skirted dress with puffy sleeves and a tight-fitting waist. "Do you like the color?" she asked. "You and the bridesmaids are all wearing teal."

116

"I love it!" She slipped the dress over her head, and Emily zipped up the back. "It's a perfect fit!" she said, as she twirled.

"Here, try on the shoes." Emily held out a pair of satin, high-heeled pumps. "They're all dyed to match."

"They're a little snug," Rosalind said as she maneuvered the shoe over her heel, "but I think they'll be okay."

Emily handed her a little pillbox hat with a small veil to complete the ensemble. Rosalind tried it on and looked in the full-length mirror attached to the back of the bedroom door.

"It's beautiful," she said approvingly. "What color will the bouquets be?"

"Mom helped me pick them out. They're coral hues with white accents. We'll pick them up at the florist's shop on the way back from the temple tomorrow."

Emily reached under the bed and pulled out the large white box that contained her wedding gown. When she opened it, the light fabric of the dress began to expand as if rising all by itself. She held it up, admiring her reflection in the mirror.

Wide-eyed, Rosalind exclaimed, "Oh, Emily, that is gorgeous! It's just the dress I would expect you to choose."

"I really wanted to keep it simple, with very little ornamentation. Notice the elegant lines? I'm thinking that with a little alteration here and there, I can wear it each time I attend the temple in the future."

Rosalind was awestruck with how truly beautiful her friend had become. The radiant expression on her face conveyed how deeply in love she was, and how much she was looking forward to her temple marriage tomorrow. Rosalind longed to know those feelings one day.

"The only thing that could possibly make it any better, is if you could be there with me," Emily said as she hugged

Rosalind. "But when you get married in the temple, I'll be there with you."

Rosalind smiled, but didn't respond. She fiercely hoped that would happen someday.

The night was interrupted several times by tiny cries from the bassinet. Her grandmother tended to the baby's needs as quickly as possible to keep her from waking the family. She wanted Hank to be able to get a good night's sleep.

But she needn't have bothered. Alone in his room, he lay awake muffling his sobs in his pillow.

CHAPTER THIRTEEN

Next morning, everyone was up before dawn. They were all in a tizzy getting breakfast out of the way, dressing, and filling cars for the drive to Salt Lake City.

Phil and Pat took Emily in their station wagon with Brian sitting beside her, and Billy and Brent in the back seat. Four small suitcases were snugly attached to the luggage carrier on the roof.

Hank started out a few minutes later in his 1966 Volkswagen van. Donald rode shotgun, and Rosalind and Carrie sat in the rear seat with the baby in a car seat between them. Scott had the middle seat all to himself.

Phil had worried that with the heavy snowfall through the night the roads might still be a little dicey for travelers. It might also make parking places scarce in the temple parking lot. But not only were the roads pretty well cleared, but the parking lot had several open spaces when the family arrived.

"Hey, how lucky can you get?" Hank said as he pulled into the lot. "There's Dad's car with room for us to park right next to him."

He pulled into the space beside the family station wagon and turned off the engine. His passengers began wrapping up to step out into the cold again. Scott scrambled out first and looked around for his brothers.

Hank said, "Carrie, wait until I get around to your side. I'll take Rose until everyone gets out."

While he was making his way around, Carrie unbuckled the car seat and gently lifted out the sleeping infant. She adjusted her tiny knitted cap, bundled her up in a yellow blanket, and carefully handed her out to Hank. Then she carefully climbed out onto the icy pavement. As Rosalind followed, a cold wind blasted her in the face.

"Hank, don't wait for us," Carrie said. "You go ahead and take Rose inside so she won't have to be in the cold so long. We'll meet you there."

Since only Phil and Pat, Hank and Emily would be able to enter the temple, Rosalind, Carrie and Rose would wait in the visitor's center with the Watson boys during the wedding ceremony.

Carrie leaned back into the van to get Rose's diaper bag. "Be careful crossing the street, boys," she called a big sister's warning to Scott and Donald who had darted ahead.

The girls were shivering from the cold and grateful to reach the warm building. Hank and his little brothers were waiting for them just inside the door.

He took charge and counted heads again to be sure everyone was present. Lifting the blanket slightly to check on the baby, he smiled faintly.

"Rosalind, would you mind keeping Rose for me?"

"I'd love to, Hank," she said as she reached out for her.

"Enjoy yourselves, girls and boys. See you after the wedding," he said as he walked out the door.

The ornate spires of the Salt Lake Temple could be seen rising against the winter gray sky through the large windows. The view was breathtaking. It was far more beautiful than all the photos in books and magazines. Rosalind had had no idea what to expect, and was certainly not disappointed.

Carrie realized this was her friend's first visit to Temple Square. "Why don't I tend the baby while you look at all the artwork and displays. Take your time.

"There's a theater that shows a beautiful film called *Man's Search For Happiness* all about the Plan of Salvation. I think you'd really like it."

"I don't want you to feel like I'm taking advantage of you," Rosalind said apologetically. "What about the boys? Will they be all right on their own?"

"Oh, sure. They'll probably spend most of the time walking around. You go ahead. We'll be sitting right over there when you get back. After you see the film, be sure to walk up that ramp over there. It leads to the most beautiful thing you've ever seen. I want to know what you think."

"Okay. Thanks, Carrie."

After wandering around, reading the descriptions of the murals and displays, Rosalind headed to the theater that was rapidly filling up. The lights went out and the screen lit up.

As she watched in rapt attention the film began with the story of a young man, then traced the cycle of life from birth to death, followed by the ultimate reunion with loved ones waiting on the other side. It warmed her heart as she thought of the passing of each of her family members who had died.

I wonder if that's what my grandfather saw? Not flowers on the wallpaper at all.

She wiped the tears from her cheeks as the lights came back on and followed the flow of the audience to the outside of the theater. She found the ramp Carrie had spoken of and headed upstairs.

Nothing prepared her for the sight that greeted her on the upper level. There stood an eleven-foot tall gleaming white replica of Bernal Thorvaldsen's celebrated statue of the "Christus." The Savior was looking downward at the visitors, the spear mark in his side, and the prints of the nails in his bare feet and down-stretched palms.

On the vaulted ceiling and all the surrounding walls stretched an enormous mural of the heavens, reminiscent of the Sistine Chapel's famous frescoes. She strolled back and forth, overcome by the vastness of the universe framing Christ's statue.

Oh! I wish Rusty were here to see this with me!

She was so caught up in the spirit that she lingered, not wanting to leave. When she returned to Carrie, Phil Watson and the boys were seated with her.

"Ah, there you are," Phil said. "What did you think? It's impressive, huh?"

"Impressive is a pretty inadequate word," Rosalind said, still dazed. "But yes, I'm impressed. I'm sorry. I lost track of the time. I hope I haven't held everyone up."

"Well, I just got here, but we'd better hurry up or we'll have a family of icicles waiting for us."

The walkways around the visitors' center and the temple had been cleared of snow. A few shivering tourists out to see the sights passed by, their warm breath puffing patterns into the cold air.

As she trudged along, Rosalind thought of dozens of questions in her mind arising from the humbling experience she had had in the visitor's center. But she decided she would wait until later to ask them. Maybe there might be time after the newlyweds were away on their honeymoon, and things had settled down at the Watson home.

When they arrived at the front face of the temple, they found the photographer finishing up pictures of the bride and groom. Emily was radiant. *It must be true what they say about brides*, Rosalind thought when she saw her best friend standing with her new husband. When the photographer gave them a break, the groom removed his suit coat and draped it over the bride's shoulders to shield her from the cold until they were ready to resume.

"Emily wants you in the family pictures," Phil said.

Rosalind stepped back and shook her head. "Well, I just thought I'd take care of Rose so Hank doesn't have to worry about her."

"Nope," Phil said. "You're a member of this family, too. And Emily wouldn't have it any other way. Besides, Hank will probably want to hold his baby in the pictures."

When the bone-chilling photo session ended, the photographer finally announced, "Okay, I think we've got it. Thank you all. I'll have proofs ready for you to review in a week or so. Now, everybody go find a warm place."

They scurried toward the parking lot and the promise of warm cars for the ride back to the Watson home. Emily held up the skirt of her wedding gown and stepped carefully while Pat gathered up the train to avoid it dragging in the wet snow.

Hank drove along in silence while Carrie and Rosalind discussed the highlights of the morning. Still feeling the sacredness of Temple Square, Donald and Scott sat together in the middle seat and talked in hushed voices of their deceased baby brother, Adam.

Emily, still beaming from the morning's events, almost

floated up to her room to change out of her wedding gown. She hung it carefully on a hanger on the bedroom door to avoid wrinkles before wearing it again tonight for the wedding reception in the cultural hall at church.

Pat had prepared a roast the night before. After changing into corduroy slacks and a comfortable sweater, she began to warm it in the oven while she and Carrie prepared the side dishes.

A few minutes later, Emily emerged from her room wearing a casual pair of jeans and a BYU sweatshirt. She started down the stairs to join the family.

"Wait! Stop right there!" Carrie said as she passed through on her way back to the kitchen.

Emily was startled. She halted precariously midway down the stairs.

"Quickly now! Before you even think about what you're going to say, do you feel any different now that you're married?" Carrie asked.

"Yes. I do feel different." Emily's smile was joyful. "Everything is different," she answered reverently.

Scott went to answer a knock on the front door and came back with Brad, who had changed clothes at his parents' home in Springville. He had come to join his bride and new in-laws for the sumptuous meal that was already being set on the table.

Hank slipped away after lunch to take a nap, and left baby Rose in the care of Rosalind and Carrie. The afternoon passed quickly to the sound of agreeable conversation and happy laughter, and soon it was time for everyone to dress for the reception.

Emily and her groom reminded Rosalind of a couple of movie stars as they stood graciously in the receiving line, flanked by both sets of parents.

Rosalind, as maid of honor, stood near Emily with the bridesmaids, while Hank, as best man, stood dutifully close to Brad along with the groomsmen. Dozens of friends and family members came to honor the couple, and passed pleasantries with them and members of the bridal party as they passed by.

Emily introduced Rosalind to the guests as her best friend. Even though everything seemed to be moving like the fast-action speed in a movie, the bride made an extra effort to introduce her to a few handsome bachelors as they came through the line.

Many guests expressed their sympathies to Hank on his loss. From time to time, Rosalind stole a glance in his direction to assure herself that he was holding up all right. A couple of times she noticed tears forming in his eyes as someone who had known the couple well stopped to say a few words to him, or offered the comfort of a hug.

Rosalind's feet were aching by the time the well-wishers stopped coming through the receiving line. Seats were filling up at the round tables arranged throughout the cultural hall.

Above the din, Phil Watson called for attention in his strongest voice. "Friends and family," he announced. "While you weren't looking, Emily and Brad made their way to the table in the back of the hall. They're about to cut the wedding cake. So please turn your attention in that direction."

As Rosalind stood nearby, Emily and Brad took the cake knife in hand and delicately cut off the first two slices. Brad respectfully picked off a bite from his plate and held it to Emily's lips. She did the same for him. No comical face-smearing for them. Rosalind remembered in their girlhood conversations, that she and Emily had agreed on that point, out of the respect and dignity they both wanted to display.

CHAPTER FOURTEEN

Glad to be out of her official duty as maid of honor, Rosalind took a seat at an empty table off to the side. A few of the eligible guys Emily had introduced, stopped by and asked her to dance. She accepted a couple of times, but discovered that, no matter what terrific dancers they were, or how good-looking, her thoughts were far away.

Now she was content to just watch the dances of the bride and groom, and the mother and son. When Phil danced with his married daughter, for a brief moment Rosalind felt sad, and maybe even a little bit envious, that she would never have that father-daughter dance.

She glanced around the room and saw Carrie shifting the baby from one arm to the other. It was surprising how tiring it could be to hold so little weight. She caught her eye and beckoned to her to come over and join her.

"I'm sure you want to enjoy the party," Rosalind said knowingly. "You go ahead. Let me take care of Rose for a while."

"Oh, thank you," Carrie said with relief. "Sure you don't mind?"

"No. I love to hold her. We're still making friends."

Grateful for the offer, Carrie handed her the baby and disappeared into a gathering of teenagers while Rosalind happily cuddled the infant. She would have been contented to spend the rest of the evening with little Rose.

She had tried hard not to show it, but the crowd of strangers was beginning to wear on her. She had smiled so much that her face muscles ached.

Her respite ended too quickly for her. All too soon Pat came to claim the sweet little bundle.

"Rosalind," she said apologetically, "we don't want to make you feel like a babysitter. Here, let me take the baby. There are some family and friends out there who have never seen her." Before she could protest, Pat took the baby into the crowd to show off her first grandchild.

Rosalind felt awkward suddenly finding herself sitting alone with nothing to do. Not until then did she realize how hungry she was. Shyly, she joined the line at the refreshments table and took a piece of cake, some cookies and nuts, and a cup of pink lemonade.

She returned to her seat, grateful for a few moments to relax. Retreating from the crowd, Hank walked up and pulled out a chair beside her.

"Rose sure is beautiful, isn't she?" he said, searching for something to talk about. "I don't know that much about young babies, but I had always heard that old joke that all newborns look like Winston Churchill." He managed a weak smile.

"Yes. She *is* beautiful, and so perfect. And I don't think she looks a bit like Winston Churchill!" She pretended offense. "You're very blessed that she's so healthy."

"Yeah. I am," he said as he smoothed his hair back from his brow. "I don't know how I'd handle it if she weren't. It's hard enough losing Crystal like that."

In the dim light of the reception hall, the dark shadows beneath his eyes seemed more prominent. Rosalind simply sat and listened. That was all she could do.

"Thank goodness for Mom and the rest of the family stepping up the way they have. I've been no help at all." He rubbed his hands together, and then examined them closely, turning the now loose gold wedding band on his finger.

"We were so excited when we found out we were having a baby. Crystal and I took childbirth classes at the hospital. In the last one they taught us how to diaper a doll," he said with a faint smile that faded into a frown.

"They didn't teach anything about how to raise a motherless infant. Like how to dress her, and fix her hair, and teach her to tie her shoes. How to listen when she needs to talk about girl stuff," he said with a touch of bitterness in his desperation.

Rosalind looked deeply into his eyes, "Things have a way of working out, Hank. Maybe not in the way we would like, or as soon as we think they should. But some day, you'll find someone else to love. Someone who will be a good mother to Rose. And maybe you'll have more children together." She knew he wasn't ready to hear that, and she worried that it came out like platitudes.

Hank shook his head emphatically. "That's not going to happen anytime soon. I'm not going back into that rat race of dating and courtship! Right now, I'm just hoping to find a good babysitter!

"Mom was planning to go back to teaching kindergarten next fall to save for missions and college for my five younger brothers. To say nothing of a wedding for Carrie. Thank goodness, Emily was smart. She worked and saved to help pay for this extravaganza, or it would have cost Mom and Dad a fortune."

He made another attempt at a smile. She searched the face of this stranger sitting beside her. And for a brief moment, Rosalind saw a glimpse of the old Hank.

They sat together in comfortable silence for a few moments, quietly entertaining their own private thoughts. Questions flashed through Rosalind's mind.

What if, when he had returned from his mission, he had chosen me instead? Would it have turned out differently? Would I be sitting here with him at Emily's wedding reception holding our baby? And would it be Rose, or a different child altogether?

It was a beautiful fantasy, but this was hard reality in the here and now. She fought off the notion. Instead, she thought of her encounter with Crystal, whether a dream or a vision, and felt a renewed desire to help Hank deal with his pain.

Some of his buddies stopped by the table to visit. They discussed old times and people she didn't know. He introduced her, but she was content to just watch him interact with them. She felt no need to participate in any of their conversations.

Just at that moment Patricia and Rose appeared at the table. Their return rescued Rosalind from an awkward situation.

"I'm not sure about you," she said to Rosalind with a warm smile, "but I'm beginning to wear out from all the whirlwind of the last few days."

"I know what you mean. And I haven't dealt with nearly as much as you have," Rosalind said as she smiled back.

Pat looked down at the sleeping infant's face. Then she looked searchingly at Rosalind and asked apologetically, "Would you mind watching the baby again for a little bit? Phil and I have to organize a cleanup party for afterwards."

"Would I? I'd love to take care of her." She took Rose into her arms.

Hank's friends had drifted away by now. He watched intently as Rosalind cradled his daughter and swayed gently to rock her. Her naturally curly brown hair reaching down to her shoulders moved gently with each motion.

Rosalind had grown more beautiful since he had last seen her. He had had no notion that she had feelings for him back then. She was just the kid from across the street, his kid sister's friend, his friend, and nothing more.

It wasn't until that Christmas vacation, when he had unthinkingly confided in her his plans to propose to Crystal, that Emily had set him straight. When his sister told him how bitterly Rosalind had wept at the news, he had felt embarrassment and remorse that he had hurt her so badly.

The bride and her groom, Brad Clifford, joined them at the table, happy to get off their feet. Emily wrapped her arms around her brother in a warm hug. She wanted so much to share her happiness with him, to warm his aching heart with her joy.

Turning to Rosalind, she took her hand. "Roz, I'm so glad you could be here to share the happiest day of my life with me."

"I can see how happy you are," she said with admiration. "If I had ever had any doubt that I wanted a temple marriage, seeing you and Brad together has cured me of that notion."

Emily was delighted at the prospect. "When you do go to the temple, let me be your escort. I'd like nothing better than to be with you when you go through for the first time, and to see you married there."

"Em," Roz said with emotion, "you are terrific. Having you for a friend has changed my life. You've been my role model and ideal since we first met. Thank you for sharing this experience with me." She leaned in closer to whisper, "I think your husband is a great choice."

Rosalind genuinely liked Brad. He and Emily complimented each other very well. It was a good match. She was biased, of course, but she felt he was a very lucky guy to win her friend. With Brad in pre-med, they had many years of schooling ahead of them, and all the challenges and struggles that time would bring.

The baby was stirring. As she awoke, she opened her eyes and stretched. Then a spreading warmth could be felt through her outfit.

Rosalind smiled in recognition. "It's time for a diaper change. I'll be right back." She excused herself and pulled the diaper bag from under the table. As she headed for the ladies' room, Hank's eyes followed her.

In her absence, Emily had a chance at last to speak with her brother. "She's still the same sweet girl from across the street, only more confident and mature. I'm so glad she was able to come out here for the wedding."

"Yeah. So am I," said Hank, still looking in the direction Rosalind had gone with the baby.

Emily continued, "I just wish she had been able to come out to the 'Y' with us instead of staying in Grayson. Especially since she's all alone back there, now that Mrs. Matthews is gone."

She reached for Brad's hand. "Maybe we should all try to talk her into transferring next year." She reached up and gave her husband a brief kiss. "We could fix her up with some handsome returned missionary, and maybe she'd get married and stay out here.

"Wouldn't it be great to raise our families together? Just think of all the holidays and family nativity pageants we could have!"

Rosalind returned with the baby, who was now letting

everyone know she wanted to be fed. Reaching into the diaper bag, she pulled out a bottle of formula and a cloth diaper. She paused before sitting down.

"Do you want to feed her, Hank?"

He glanced up for a moment, and then awkwardly reached up for the baby. Rosalind shook the prepared Playtex nurser bottle, removed the cap, pushed up on the disposable plastic bag inside to release any air, and passed it to him. Then she smiled and draped a burp cloth over the shoulder of his new suit.

The baby turned her head from side to side in the rooting reflex, hungrily trying to latch on to the large nipple with her tiny mouth. Once she had found it, she gave a sigh and sucked peacefully. Hank looked triumphantly at Rosalind, and then at Emily, and his new brother-in-law.

When Rose looked up into her father's eyes, he was suddenly aware of a new sensation, that biological recognition of a connection between parent and child, as he felt her total dependence on him. Enveloped in a sense of peace and fulfillment, his love for her expanded, and filled his wounded heart.

Rosalind leaned forward with a tissue and blotted the trail of formula as it leaked from the corners of the baby's mouth. Hank looked up and smiled, relaxing into his new role as father and protector.

Rosalind smiled back at him with understanding and support. At that moment she could see a light penetrating the deep depression that had entrapped him.

Hank was going to be okay. He was going to be a wonderful father.

CHAPTER FIFTEEN

During the traditional tossing of the bridal bouquet, Rosalind hung back, not wanting to participate in the competition. It was caught by one of the excited bridesmaids. When Brad launched the bride's garter like a slingshot, Hank stepped aside to make room for the tallest groomsman, who snatched it from the air.

Soon after, Emily and Brad departed to spend their first night together at the Hotel Utah. Tomorrow, once the roads heading south were cleared, they would leave on their honeymoon trip to Flagstaff for a couple of days of skiing, then on to Phoenix and Tucson.

When the cleanup was done, everyone else in the family returned home. After the last couple of weeks of frantic hyperactivity, the Watsons were in various states of exhaustion. They dispersed to their rooms to change clothes and relax.

Soon they began to gather in the family room. After some lazy small talk Rosalind said, "Sister Watson you must be the most tired of all of us. So I'm going to take the baby and her bassinet to my room, and give you and Brother Watson a chance to get some sleep."

"Oh, Rosalind," Pat objected, "you're our guest. You've already done enough. I can't let you become the nanny."

"Well, Brother Watson said that I'm a member of this family, too. And I sure feel like it. So don't be selfish with Rose. Let me take care of her tonight and you just rest. Okay?"

"Okay," Pat surrendered. "I do need that. And thank you so much."

ရှ౭

Rosalind fed the baby in front of the fireplace at two o'clock in the morning. Then she sat and stared into the faintly glowing embers, thinking nothing in particular, as she gently rocked Rose back to sleep.

Getting out of the squeaky rocker as carefully as she could, she tiptoed back upstairs to Emily's room. She didn't see Hank watching from his doorway.

The baby awoke for another feeding about four o'clock. She took longer to fall asleep this time. Rosalind continued to hold her on her shoulder even after a couple of burps.

Rose bobbed her little head unsteadily to turn and look into the face of the one holding her. It was astonishing how familiar her gaze was. *She really does have Hank's eyes.* Still, Rosalind saw a definite resemblance to her mother, Crystal.

Quiet footsteps drew her attention. Hank took a seat beside her and leaned forward with his elbows on his knees. He clasped his hands and watched the two of them.

"I'm sorry, Hank," Rosalind whispered. "I hope I didn't bother you. I tried not to wake anyone, but I had to warm the bottle. Your daughter was a little more impatient this time."

Hank smiled sleepily. "That's okay. I'm grateful for your

help. She seems to really like you," he whispered back.

"I think she likes anyone who feeds her," Rosalind joked.

"Are you seeing anyone in Grayson?"

Rosalind was taken by surprise at the question. Considering it carefully for a moment, she answered it truthfully.

"No. There's no one in Grayson."

She didn't volunteer anything more. It felt disloyal discussing Rusty with Hank. Or was it the other way around?

"Emily sure wishes you would transfer out here to BYU." He didn't mention that he wished it also. "We used to have such fun hanging out during high school," he paused. "Back before life got so complicated."

"Look, Hank," she gazed deeply into his eyes. "I'm sure you have wonderful memories of times with Crystal. Even if it's too painful to think of them right now, you can put them away for a little while, and they'll still be there for you. Just as she will.

"I know she's looking down on you and Rose, and watching over you both. She would want you to be happy, Hank, and to give your daughter a wonderful life."

Hank looked down at the baby nestled in Rosalind's arms. "You're right, Roz. It's just that I'm having a tough time getting used to the way life has changed. It still seems like such a bad dream."

৩৯৫৩

Most of the family had chosen to sleep in the next day. Hank had awakened when he heard baby noises coming from Emily's room where Rosalind lay sleeping.

137

While she got up and changed Rose's diaper, he went to the kitchen and made a bottle of formula, all by himself. He was waiting for them when they came downstairs to the living room.

"Breakfast is served." He took his daughter from her.

"Oh, good," Rosalind said in relief. "I've got some packing to do."

On the way back to Emily's room, she passed a sleepy Carrie, rubbing her eyes and yawning, as she headed down the steps.

"Hank! You've got this?" she asked in surprise as she saw her brother feeding Rose.

"Sure, Sis. Nothing to it." He smiled down as the baby studied his face in curiosity.

$$\circ\!\!\sim\!\!\circ$$

Rosalind had said her goodbyes to the rest of the Watson family after breakfast. As she zipped up her purse, she saw her grandmother's keys, and they reminded her of the lonely house in Grayson.

Her plane was scheduled to leave at one o'clock that afternoon. Hank carried her bags out to his van and turned on the engine so the heater could warm up.

"Thanks for babysitting so I can drive Roz to the airport, Mom," he said.

"Don't worry about a thing," his mother answered. "Just think of it as another chance for me to spend quality grandmother time with her. You drive carefully, Hank."

Pat walked out to the driveway to give Rosalind one last hug. "I'm so glad you could be with us for the wedding. I know it meant the world to Emily. Take good care of yourself, and stay in touch. If there's ever anything we can do for you, just let us know. And if you do decide to transfer out here to school, we'll be ready to help!" she encouraged.

"Thank you, Sister Watson," Rosalind said, wondering just how far this idea of her transferring had gone through the Watson family. "Give Emily and Brad a hug for me when they get back from their honeymoon."

Hank had been holding the car door open for her. Once she had climbed into the van, he gave his mother a short hug and a kiss on the cheek. Then they were off.

They had been on the road for a few minutes before either of them spoke. Then Hank said, "I'm sorry you won't be here tomorrow to attend church with us."

"I'm sorry, too. But I need to get home to rest up before going back to work Monday."

"You mean the library is open over the holidays?" he asked in surprise.

"No. Christmas break doesn't start until Tuesday, the twenty-third. I ditched my Thursday and Friday classes so I could be here for the wedding."

"Oh, yeah. I guess I've lost track of time." He felt a little embarrassed when he realized the world had been going on around him while he had been caught up in his sadness.

"What are you majoring in?" he asked.

"History, with a minor in Secondary Education. But I think I'd like to go on to get a Master's Degree in Library Science. I really enjoy my work, and I think I would prefer it over teaching."

"That's great!" he exclaimed. "BYU has an excellent program in Library Science. You can even take some of the prerequisites as electives in your undergraduate program if you transfer."

"I don't know, Hank." She felt overwhelmed by the idea. "It sure gets cold out here!" She laughed as she shivered and pulled her coat tightly around her.

"You'd get used to it," he said as he turned up the van's heater. "That's what popcorn and hot chocolate are for, at least at the Watson house."

She changed the subject. "It's been really great seeing all of you again. Carrie seems so much happier out here."

"Yeah, it was a good move for her. She's gained a lot of self-confidence, and has become much more out-going at church.

"Crystal and I have been attending one of the BYU student wards. I guess I'll transfer back to Mom and Dad's ward now. I may move back home with them at the end of the month, since Rose and I will be spending most of our time over there anyway."

"That's probably a good idea for a while. You'd have a lot of help with the baby, and it would be good for her to grow up in a big family like you and Emily did."

The conversation lagged for a few minutes.

"Don't you ever get lonely back there, all alone, rattling around in that old house? I mean, it's a nice house and all, but it's so big for just one person." Hank tried to pick his way carefully through this conversation.

"Sometimes I do."

She looked out the window at the whiteness blanketing the expansive mountainous countryside. Her thoughts turned again to the empty house awaiting her return. She closed her eyes and leaned her head against the passenger side window.

Where exactly is home now? This frozen place seems so foreign to me.

She had no doubt that the Watsons would take her in. They might even rent her a room to share with Carrie.

Maybe someday Hank might want to marry again. She knew she would never hold first place in his heart, as he had in hers. But maybe she could settle for that. They could still have a good life together.

She compared their situation to that of Rusty and Charlene. He would always be in second place too, and without a temple marriage.

She had driven these thoughts out of her mind by the time they arrived at the airport. Hank had assumed that she had fallen asleep, and he had driven in silence the rest of the trip.

They pulled up at the passenger departure curb, and he touched her shoulder to rouse her. "Hey, we're here."

Rosalind looked up and smiled at him. She unbuckled her seatbelt, and gathered her purse and ticket.

"It's not too late to decide to stay for a little while longer," he said wistfully.

"I've enjoyed the visit, Hank. But I really need to get back." She smiled sweetly.

"Well, at least give us a call when you get home to let us know you got there safely."

"I will."

Hank carried her bags in for her, and waited with her at the gate until they announced boarding for her flight. He looked at her with tear-filled eyes. Then he gathered her into a desperate hug, clinging to this neighbor girl as if she still lived just across the street.

"I'll miss you, Roz. I hope you'll come back out to see us. And that you'll really consider transferring."

Rosalind held him tightly and kissed his cheek.

"Goodbye, Hank. Take care of yourself. Hug little Rose for me every day."

"I will. Write to me sometime."

"Send me pictures." She smiled and blew him a kiss as she walked through the gate.

One more thing to consider.

CHAPTER SIXTEEN

Rosalind turned on the living room light of the Matthews house, and closed the front door behind her. It was good to be back home again. Yet, she couldn't help thinking she was beginning to treat Grayson as a layover between travels. She now felt torn between two universes, the neutral zone being here at this house where she had grown up.

After settling in, Rosalind sat at the desk in her bedroom. She took out a sheet of notebook paper and drew a line down the middle. Remembering an exercise from her Marriage and Family class, she labeled the two columns "Hank" and "Rusty."

Under the headings of each, she wrote "Pros", and halfway down the length of the page, she wrote "Cons." She worked for almost an hour, adding ideas as they came to her.

Under the heading for Hank she wrote:

Pros:

• He loves me like a sister.

- I love him.
- He's LDS.
- He can take me to the temple.
- I love his family.
- He's loving and kind.
- He has a child, and may someday want more.
- He's a good father
- We have fun together

Cons:

- He might never ask me to marry him.
- I would always be second to Crystal in his heart.

Under the heading for Rusty, she wrote:

Pros:

- He loves me, and only me.
- I love him.
- He's LDS.
- Maybe someday he will take me to the temple.
- I love his family
- He's loving and kind.
- He wants children.
- He'd be a good father.
- We have fun together
- I would always come first with him.

Cons:

- He might not stay active in the Church.
- He might never take me to the temple.

Finishing the exercise only convinced her that life was full of uncertainties. Of that much she was certain. She laughed as she analyzed that thought—the certainty of uncertainty.

✥

Christmas break was already here, and Rosalind still hadn't done any holiday decorating. Even the thought of it brought a cloud of sadness as she remembered those happy years she and her grandmother had spent together, and those good times she had shared with the Watson and Dobson families.

Somehow, decorating for one person just didn't seem like much fun. It was a lot of work, with no one to share it. Maybe she would just skip it this year.

There would be a Christmas party at the ward. She looked forward to seeing all her little ones from the nursery as they met Santa Claus in the cultural hall.

One day, an overstuffed envelope from Utah arrived in the mail. It contained a Christmas card signed by all the Watsons, and snapshots from Emily's wedding reception.

The wonderland created by the lights and decorations brought back the magical feelings she had shared with her friends. Emily and Brad looked so in love as they danced.

There were some photos of Rose with her grandmother and Aunt Carrie, and some with each of her young uncles, her dad, and one of her in Rosalind's arms.

The pictures of Hank revealed his suffering that night, the raw pain he was going through just to be there for his sister, trying to be happy for her. It was hard to even look at those. She put them at the bottom of the stack.

Emily had promised to call on Christmas Day. Rosalind looked forward to hearing all about the family's annual Christmas Eve nativity pageant. Rose would no doubt debut in the starring role of the Baby Jesus.

She received a large manila envelope from Florida the day before Christmas. It was a homemade card made of green construction paper on which was glued an enlarged photo of John and Evelyn dressed as Mr. and Mrs. Claus. Beside them stood Rusty wearing an elf hat over his Marine Corps baseball cap, and sporting pointy-toed slippers.

They all stood before a huge decorated pine tree in the window of the river house. It was draped with paper chains and tinsel, candy canes, one with a bite out of it, and tole painted stocking ornaments. The best Christmas decoration of all was the happy smiles on their faces.

They had each written a message and signed it. John's was in the biggest handwriting of all, "Just see what you're missing!"

Evelyn wrote, "Wish you could be here for Christmas. Maybe next year."

Rusty's message was particularly short for one who made his living as a newspaperman. "Miss you. Love, Rusty," he scrawled.

Rosalind placed it on the piano to enjoy whenever she was feeling the holiday blues.

On Christmas morning, she got up late. Still in her pajamas and slippers, she lingered over a breakfast of cold cereal and a banana. She could almost feel Grace's disapproval.

Sorry, Grandma.

If anyone had had to endure a solitary existence it was her grandmother, alone all those years without her husband

and son.

I hope I made a difference when I came to live with you.

Determined to mend her ways, she washed her dishes and wiped the table. It was time to get dressed, and try to make the best of her day.

Later in the morning, Rosalind sat at her grandfather's big roll top desk, studying a framed portrait of her grandmother taken shortly before last Easter. How grateful she was to have it. She daydreamed about times past, and wondered about times yet to come.

The doorbell rang, bringing her part way back. It rang again. She got up to answer. There was a man on the porch. While she was trying to decide whether to open the door, she saw he was wearing a U.S. Navy uniform.

A familiar face smiled at her. She instantly recognized her mysterious visitor as Mark William Dobson.

Opening the door, she said, "Why, Mark, where have you been? How long has it been since I saw you last?"

He just stood there, grinning.

Finally, Rosalind's thoughts caught up with her. "My goodness, Mark. Come in. Where are my manners?"

When he stepped through the door, she threw her arms around him and gave him a hug, which he tenuously returned. He was more fit than the last time she had seen him, and his frame was more filled out.

"Come on in. Have a seat."

He stood back to let her lead the way, then followed her in and sat beside her on the couch.

"Tell me about yourself. How are you? And tell me about your mother. I haven't heard a thing."

She stopped and laughed at her jumbled questions. "I'm sorry. I haven't given you a chance to get a word in edgewise."

Well," he drawled, "I don't know just where to begin."

"Start with your mother," Rosalind suggested. "The last I heard, she went up to visit your sister in North Carolina. I've been waiting ever since for her to come back."

"Mom's still up there with Teena and her family," Mark William said. "I guess there was no way for you to know, but Mom had a stroke several weeks ago."

"Oh, no!" Rosalind was alarmed. "Is she all right?"

"It affected that part of her brain that governs speech, and she has trouble talkin'. Can you imagine? My mother havin' trouble talkin'?" he laughed softly. "But that doesn't mean she doesn't keep tryin'." He rolled his eyes.

"What's the prognosis? Is she getting any better?" Rosalind asked with concern.

"Yeah. Probably. But it's very slow. I don't think she'll ever be the same again. She also has trouble gittin' around, and has to use a cane.

"I stopped by up there to spend my Christmas leave, and asked if I could borrow her car to drive down here to check on the house," he said. Then, after a slight pause, he added, "And to see you."

Rosalind glanced out the living room window to the street where Mark William had parked Muriel's car. It looked like a long lost friend sitting there.

"Oh, Mark. I'm so sorry to hear about your mother. Be sure to give me her address so I can write to her."

"I'm sure she'd love to hear from you, Rosalind. She really loved you and your grandma."

He took a small notepad and a ballpoint pen from the pocket of his pea coat. "Let me give it to you now, or I'll forget." He wrote quickly, tore out the page and handed it to her.

"Thanks," she said and laid the note on the coffee table. "Now, tell me about yourself. How long have you been in the Navy?"

He gave her a smile that belied his pride. "I joined up about seven months ago. After your grandma died, I did a lot of thinkin' about what a son of a...", he caught himself in time, "a stinker I had been. I treated my mother somethin' awful, and I didn't even know why.

"Your grandma was always so good to me. She and my mom were such close friends. The more I thought about it, the worse I felt," he confessed.

"We were all so worried about you, Mark, and wondered what was going to become of you. The way you wear that uniform, I'd say you've got your life straightened out now, right?"

"Yeah, I have," he said slowly, straightening his shoulders. "But it wasn't easy, and it wasn't quick.

"After your grandma's funeral, I took off again on my bike. I rode down to Florida and on down through the Keys, then back up the coast to Maine. I worked all kinds of odd jobs for food and lodgin' money along the way.

"I quit drinkin'. The more I thought about that crowd I'd fallen in with here at home, the more I realized that they sure weren't my friends. They were really draggin' me down. I felt guilty about the way I had treated everyone." His apology was sincere.

"I'm so glad to hear this, Mark." She reached out and laid her hand on his.

"Thank you," he said looking down at their hands. "I'm just sorry it took so long for me to straighten up.

"I stayed in Maine three or four weeks and then decided to head south again. When I reached North Carolina, I decided to give my sister a phone call just to say hi. She said Mom was visitin', and she put her on the phone. I asked her if I could come down and see her. She said sure, they'd both be glad to see me. I just wanted to say I was sorry, and ask her to forgive me."

As he told his story, Rosalind could almost see in him the confused young boy she had first met when she came to live in Grayson. She felt sorry for him and the years he had wasted.

"So did she? Forgive you, I mean," Rosalind asked kindly.

"Sure she did. We both cried a lot. Teena let us have our time together while she was out in the kitchen cookin' up a great supper for us.

"We had a good visit. I stayed with 'em for a couple of days. Then I hit the road again headin' north. I passed through Norfolk, and saw all the Navy ships. It was pretty excitin'.

"I rode over to a motorcycle shop and sold my bike. Well, I almost gave it away. But I didn't care. I walked across the street, and had a meal at a café.

"While I was eatin', I looked out the window, and saw a recruitin' station down the street. Then, all of a sudden, I knew what I had to do. When I finished eatin', I walked over there and joined up. It's one of the best decisions I ever made."

Rosalind looked at him with approval and affection. "I think you're right," she said.

Here he sat before her, a different, and much better person than the Mark William she had last seen. His red hair was cut short, and his freckles, though still there, were fading. His shoulders were broader, and there was an air of confidence about him. Yes, the military had been good for him.

"So what do you do in the Navy?" she asked. "You have the look of a man who does important work."

"Ha!" he laughed. "But I am learnin' some important stuff. Most of what I've done so far is go to school. Almost anything I want to learn, the Navy is willin' to teach me. I'm goin' to train now to be a radar man."

"Do you think you'll make a career out of the Navy?"

"Too early to tell," he answered. "I like it all right. But I think I'd like to go to college. Study physics or math, maybe.

"Can you believe that? I never mixed too well with science. But I've got time to make up my mind. And then there's that little matter of the war in Vietnam. So, we'll see how things go. I'm signed up for four years. I don't even have one down yet."

"I'm so proud of you, Mark. And I know your mother is, too," Rosalind said sincerely through happy tears.

"Well, I've been keepin' up with you, Rosalind. I know you're a student down at Grayson College. I always knew you were goin' places."

"Going places?" She laughed. "I'm still here in Grayson, and wondering what I'm going to do with the rest of my life."

"Well, look, I wasn't completely honest with you when I said I had come to Grayson to check on the house. Mostly, I came to check on you. I'm passin' through pretty quick, though. So look, would you like to go out with me for a bite to eat and a cup of coffee? No, wait. Forget the coffee. I know you don't drink that stuff. But I'll buy you a soda or a milk shake. How 'bout it? I noticed there's a new restaurant up by the highway."

Rosalind regarded him for a moment. He was beginning to think she was going to say no again. But she surprised him.

"I'd love to. And it'll be fun to ride in your mother's old car again. Besides, it seems to me you owe me a milk shake. Remember that first summer we met?"

He laughed. "Of course I remember. There I was at the drug store with a pocket full of stolen candy, wonderin' how I could put it back without gettin' caught. Then you knocked your milk shake over. When it crashed onto the floor, everybody looked at you, and it saved me from maybe goin' to jail" he chuckled.

"Well, okay then. Let's go, so you can finally pay your debt to society."

CHAPTER SEVENTEEN

"Thank you for a wonderful lunch, Mark," Rosalind said. "I've never tried that place before, but the food was so delicious, I'm sure I'll go back."

"I'm glad you had a good time. I was afraid you were going to turn me down again," he said sheepishly, stuffing his hands into his pockets.

"I can't tell you how proud I am of you! I wish Grandma could see you in your uniform. She always had faith in you, you know."

"Well, I sure made it hard for her, not to mention my mother, and you. Thanks for not givin' up on me, Rosalind. You've been a good friend."

"Would you like to come inside for a while? You've got a long drive ahead of you."

"No thanks. You're right, though. I do have a long drive.

"Thanks for not holdin' all that stuff I did against me, Rosalind. I'm what Pastor Jackson used to call a 'penitent.' I'm sorry, and I'm tryin' hard to change my life," he said sincerely.

Rosalind's eyes brimmed with tears, and she reached up and gave her friend a hug. He responded appropriately in a brotherly manner, so she kissed his cheek.

"Well, I'd better get goin' now," he said self-consciously. "I'll give my mom your message. She'll be glad to know you're gittin' along all right."

"You drive carefully, Mark," she said. "And please stay in touch because we'll always be good friends."

He turned without another word. Rosalind stood on the porch watching, and waved one last time as he drove out of sight.

She stood for a while reflecting on their visit, and thinking to herself that he was becoming the man her grandmother had always thought him capable of.

People really can change.

As she unlocked the front door, she heard the kitchen phone ringing. She quickly tossed her purse on the foyer table and rushed to answer it.

"Hello, Roz? It's Carrie. Merry Christmas!"

"Carrie, it's so good to hear from you! How is everyone?"

"Just fine. We're all here, and everybody wants to talk to you," the teenager answered. "Are you doing okay?"

"I'm fine, too."

Rosalind quickly filled her in on her trip back home from Utah, and the very little that had been happening. She started to mention Mark William's visit, but thought better of it, since his and Carrie's relationship had been so star-crossed and unpleasant.

Carrie's brothers took their turns saying hello. Then Pat Watson came to the phone.

"Hi, Rosalind. Are you having a good Christmas? We sure miss you. Emily, the ole married lady, is just fine. She

154

and Brad are here for dinner. I'll put her on in a minute. I just wanted to make sure you're doing okay."

"I'm doing great, Sister Watson. I'm on break from school and the library right now. It's a little boring with so much time on my hands. But it's a good chance to catch up on a lot of things I've wanted to work on. Like genealogy, for one."

After a few more words of small talk, Pat put Phil on the line. He repeated what the rest of the family had said. They were concerned about Rosalind, and wished her the best.

Hank was next, and spent his time mostly encouraging Rosalind to transfer to BYU. "Little Rose sends her love. She misses you. Bye."

Rosalind suspected that what Hank actually meant was that *he* missed her. The thought did not excite her as it once might have.

Then came Emily. "Roz! Are you having a good Christmas?"

"Yes. It's just a little quiet."

Rosalind instantly regretted her choice of words. Emily immediately seized the opening.

"Then come on out here to be with us. We all want you to. We've discussed it, and Mom and Dad would love for you to stay here with them. She would help you get transferred and registered. It could be like old times."

There it was again. It was time to lay this to rest.

"Emily, it can't be like old times," Rosalind said kindly. "You're married, and Hank is raising Rose. As much as I would like to have things the way they were in the past, we all have different lives now.

"I'd like to stay here at Grayson College and finish my History degree. Maybe then I can look at other options. But for now, I have a sense of direction that I feel good about."

Emily was disappointed. She knew in her heart that her old friend was right, but she continued anyway.

"But Roz, I don't like to think of you being all alone back there."

"I'm not alone, Emily. I have school and my work at the library," she insisted.

"I know, Roz. But except for the ward members, you don't have anybody. Or do you? Is there someone special in your life?" She spoke as though she had never even considered that possibility.

Rosalind wasn't ready to talk about her relationship with the O'Connors. Besides, she hadn't made up her mind yet about accepting Rusty's proposal.

"No. There's nobody special here in Grayson," she said. "If that changes, you'll be the first one I tell." She laughed.

"I didn't mean to pry," Emily said. "I just want you to know that we all love you, and want you to be happy. Please don't ever forget us. You're still my best friend.

"Well, I'd better go," Emily said regretfully. "The family is getting ready to open Christmas presents. Write to me. I love you, Roz. Goodbye."

"I will," Rosalind said. "I love you, too, Emily. And I love your family. Merry Christmas!"

"Merry Christmas," Emily said longingly, and hung up the phone.

Well there, did I just burn a bridge?

ക്ക

For the rest of the afternoon, she browsed through her high school yearbooks. Everyone looked so young back then. She looked so young back then.

Next she reached for her photo album on the coffee table. As she turned the pages, she especially looked for images of a young Mark William Dobson and his mother. There were several pictures taken when he was younger, but none during his troubled teenaged years. There was one of her grandmother with Muriel Dobson, taken not long before that Easter when Grace passed away.

She had forgotten about it. Now she pulled it out, and planned to look for a small picture frame. It should go on the piano, where she would be able to enjoy it more often. Maybe she could have a copy made for Muriel, and one for Mark.

Realizing that Christmas Day was slipping away. On a whim, she lifted the seat of the piano bench, and sifted through the sheet music stored there. She found a faded copy of "Rudolph the Red-Nosed Reindeer" with her father's boyish signature. There were also copies of "Frosty the Snowman" and "I'll Be Home For Christmas." She pulled them out, and sat down to play.

It had been a long time since she had tried to sight-read music, and there were many missed notes. But she didn't care. This felt more like Christmas than anything else she had done all day.

Then she reached for the LDS hymnal on the top of the piano, and searched for the section of Christmas hymns. She was more familiar with these, and began to sing along as she played.

The hours passed, and the glow of the sunset was beginning to fade. Christmas was almost over. She closed the hymnal, and carefully put away the old sheet music. If she started practicing sooner next year, she should be able to play it perfectly.

Next year. Where will I celebrate Christmas next year? Utah? Florida? Or right here in Grayson?

As night fell, she realized there were no holiday leftovers for dinner. No Christmas cookies. Not even a fruitcake.

She looked through the kitchen cabinets, trying to pick out something easy for supper. A can of tuna caught her eye, and she settled on a tuna fish sandwich.

One of her favorite movies, *Holiday Inn*, starring Bing Crosby and Fred Astaire, would be coming on TV at eight. The idea of eating her Christmas sandwich, and watching a great musical, appealed to her.

Yeah, I'm okay. For now

CHAPTER EIGHTEEN

It was the middle of winter in the South Carolina Piedmont. Classes had started again, and Rosalind was back at work in the library. She studied hard, and spent nearly all her spare time keeping up her correspondence with Emily and Brad, the Watsons, an occasional letter to Hank, a weekly letter to Mark William Dobson, one to his mother, Muriel in North Carolina, and of course, one to the O'Connors. As for Rusty, they mostly exchanged scenic picture postcards instead of letters.

Evelyn kept her up-to-date on how Rusty and John were doing, as well as on her own activities. Her letters were more informative now than they had been before Rosalind's fall visit to Adrian.

Although nothing had been said when she was visiting with the O'Connors at Thanksgiving, Rusty had actually told his parents, soon after his baptism, that he had joined the Church of Jesus Christ of Latter-day Saints in August. Now that the holidays were over, Evelyn and John occasionally visited the Tampa Ward with him, and she continued to attend Relief Society work meetings with

Charlene. They both enjoyed spending time with Russell when his mother came to visit.

In Rosalind's letters to Rusty's mother, she allowed her most important question to go unasked. Are Charlene and Rusty still dating?

She knew it didn't really matter. She had nothing to fear on that account, at least for now. Rusty would wait for her answer, and she would wait for Rusty to know of a certainty about the Gospel.

৩৯৯৩

In mid-January, Muriel's daughter, Teena, drove down from North Carolina to load up her mother's things. She was getting the house ready to rent out.

Though Teena had already married and had a family long before fourteen-year-old Rosalind had arrived in Grayson, the two of them now quickly became friends. Rosalind invited her to have dinner with her that first evening.

After the meal, they settled into a friendly conversation as they sat at the small table in the kitchen.

"It's good to be in this lovely old house again," Teena said. "We all loved your grandma and grandpa. My mama didn't have a better friend than Grace Matthews."

"I know. Grandma loved your mother. I think they were more like sisters than just friends. I'm so sorry to hear about her health problems. Is she doing any better?"

"She's still having trouble speaking, and she's pretty slow," Teena replied. "You wouldn't know her, Rosalind. She has lost a lot of weight. Part of that is because of the stroke, but the doctor has her on a strict diet, too. I think after Daddy left, she just overate to compensate for her heartache."

"But she was such a good woman," Rosalind said. "She was always at the church, helping out. I'll never forget her leading her choir," she said with a smile. "She was like a professional."

"Yes, she was. She still likes to sit on the couch at home, and hum along as I play the piano."

"Oh, do you play? That's wonderful. I'm sure she enjoys it."

"Mama made sure we kids had piano lessons. Except for Mark William," Teena said with a touch of sadness in her voice. "He didn't have much of a chance, being born so late."

"Well, you know, he was my first friend in Grayson. It was sad to see him lose his way. But I'm so glad he's doing better now. Did he tell you that he came to see me on Christmas Day?"

"He told us he wanted to check on the house, but we knew that he was really coming to see you. I'll bet you didn't know that he used to have a crush on you." She laughed.

Rosalind pretended surprise and joined in the laughter. She was sure that Teena and Mrs. Dobson had no idea just how serious that crush had been, or how long it had lasted.

"I'm so proud of him now. He's a fine-looking sailor. We had lunch together that day, and he mainly talked about your mother, and his life in the Navy."

There, I avoided that pretty well.

Changing the subject Rosalind asked, "Are you planning to move everything up to North Carolina?"

"No, I'll probably sell or donate most of the furniture. But there are some pieces she wants, so I'll rent a truck. If Mark William can get a few days leave, he'll come down and drive it for me. If he can't, my husband will catch a bus to Grayson, and drive the truck back. Getting everything ready is going to be lot of work."

Thinking of the young men in the Grayson Ward, Rosalind offered, "I think I can get some of my friends at church to help you load the truck when you're ready. And I'll try to be as much help as I can to help you pack, between classes and work."

"That would be terrific!" Teena said with relief.

Within a week, the house was empty and the truck loaded. Mark William hadn't been able to get leave, so Teena's husband was behind the wheel of the rental truck as it pulled away. Then she and Rosalind said goodbye to each other, just as if they had been life-long friends.

By the end of January, Teena's real estate agent had rented the house to a very nice older couple, and one of their grown sons who still lived at home. The new neighbors were reliable tenants, kept up the yard and took good care of the place.

❧

Rosalind and Teena began corresponding regularly, and although Rosalind still wrote a letter to Muriel every week or two, she knew that Mrs. Dobson was in no condition to write back.

Teena's letters were a good way to keep track of Muriel's health. The news was that she was making slow progress with her speech therapy, but seemed to be getting along pretty well otherwise. Teena said her mother always looked forward to receiving Rosalind's letters, and to please keep on writing.

In February a large manila envelope arrived from her Aunt Sue in New Mexico. Inside were two 8 x 10 copies of

Colonel Wesley Martin's military portrait, and one of his wedding picture with his bride, Bonnie Marie Hudson. Sue had also sent a snapshot of the gravestones of Wesley and Bonnie, side by side in the Albuquerque cemetery.

Rosalind found that one especially touching. The family marker said simply, "Martin." A couple of spaces beneath the name were the words, "Together Forever." Two simple headstones, one for Bonnie and a smaller one for Wesley Martin, had the basic gravestone information: names, birth and death dates.

Rosalind treasured the photos of her grandfather especially. She considered it a blessing that she had been able to meet him in the last few moments of his life.

She studied the photos closely, trying to see the old man in the face of the young soldier. She wondered how he had been lost for all those years, right there in the town where he had married, and raised his daughters. Time had taken much of his identity, but there was something about the eyes that she recognized.

She framed two of the photos of her grandfather, and packaged up the third to mail to Miss Lottie Maud Leonard. She enclosed an enlargement of the best of the snapshots she had taken of the pocket watch. It would be wonderful to see them on display in the museum the next time she went down to Adrian. She was certain there would be another trip, one way or the other. Rosalind paused to ponder her life's direction.

I've come so far in the past six years, from not knowing who I was or where I belonged, to knowing I had parents who loved me, and took me to the temple to be sealed to them for eternity, to having grandparents who had also received those ordinances, to having others who still may.

She was overcome with gratitude for the Plan of Salvation, for the Savior's Atonement, for her testimony, and for the blessings of the temple. Just then an image of her grandmother Grace's smiling face came into her mind. She felt an overwhelming closeness to her, as though she were wrapped in her embrace.

Thank you, Grandma, for all you gave me, and for your love.

After that experience, and realizing that she was the last of the family line, Rosalind set aside some time to do a little family history work. She dug out the old letters and records on the Matthews and Wharton sides of the family, and reviewed her old high school family history project. She made certain that current family group sheets and pedigree charts were completed fully and accurately, and with correct documentation.

Turning to her mother's line, she spread out her research before her on the dining room table. Rusty was always in the back of her mind, but she felt him especially near as she held his hand-written notes from the courthouse in Tampa.

Had he received his answer?

He was in her every prayer. And so were Hank and baby Rose.

ॐ

Pat Watson sent snapshots of how fast her first grandbaby was growing. Rose still resembled her dad. In the sequence of photos, she could see that Hank had regained a little weight, and was looking much better.

He had moved back in with his parents, and with the savings on rent and food, he had been able to stay in school full-time. The whole family pitched in, juggling their schedules to help with daycare while he worked half-days and took classes around his job. He was still on track to graduate with the Class of 1972, the same year Rosalind and Emily would receive their Bachelor's degrees.

Emily was still majoring in Elementary Education, hoping to teach kindergarten upon graduation. Rosalind had stuck with her history major. But if her education courses had taught her anything, it was that she definitely didn't want to teach.

Library Science was the way to go, she had decided. Her experiences with genealogical research, and her relationship with Miss Leonard, had given her a real desire to do archival work, preservation, and cataloging.

Rusty sent a postcard with the picture of the newly opened Adrian Historical Society and Museum. In the message area of the card, he had scrawled, "Miss Leonard sends her best regards!"

She put it into an empty Whitman's Sampler chocolates box with all his others: a postcard showing the Hillsborough County Courthouse, cards with herds of cattle, colorful blooming hibiscus plants, cowboys, horses, a rodeo parade, docks on the river, and even a view of the main street in downtown Adrian, with the newspaper office in the foreground. She treasured each one.

In return, she had sent postcards of the Grayson College campus buildings, the city library, historical sights of the region, scenic views of the mountains, and a card featuring downtown Grayson, in which could be seen Myra's beauty shop and Snow's Jewelry Store. On the back of the postcards, she sometimes wrote scriptural references and quotes that she had come across in her daily personal study, that she wanted to share with him.

She still wrote to Hank, and signed her letters, "Love, Always." But the content was always the same: how were he and Rose getting along?

She could feel things changing. Part of it was her maturity, and the way she saw the world around her. Outgrowing her first crush had led to a deeper caring and concern for Hank and his daughter. But none of that was comparable to the stirrings she felt when she thought of Rusty.

One Sunday in early March, the phone rang. She answered on the second ring, and was greeted by a familiar voice.

"Hi, Roz. This is Hank."

She was surprised and pleased, but not as thrilled as she once would have been. There was a pleasant change in his voice. He sounded happier, more at peace. It was a good sound.

"Hey, Hank," she replied. "You sound great. How are you?"

"Well, I'm doing much better than the last time we talked. I think I'm making progress. I still miss Crystal, but it isn't killing me any more. And, of course, I have little Emily Rose. She's doing great, by the way, and growing like a weed."

"I'm so glad to hear you're doing better. Everyone was so worried about you, but we have great faith in you as well. I know you'll be fine."

"Roz, I've called about a familiar subject," he started.

Rosalind knew exactly where this was going. He wanted to know if she was going to move to Utah.

"I'm speaking for everyone, but especially for Emily. Have you made up your mind about transferring out to BYU next year?"

"No. I haven't thought that much about it, Hank. I know that probably sounds a little wishy-washy, but I am pretty much tied down here. And I'm not unhappy with my job and my school work."

"Well, look, Roz. I don't mean to push you . . . "

Rosalind interrupted before he could finish, "Oh, yes you do," she said with a laugh. "But you're awfully nice about it. Thanks."

"It's not just me," he said. "We all want you to come out: Mom and Dad, Emily and Brad, Carrie, the boys…everybody. And look, you need to apply soon, and make preparations."

There was a sense of urgency in his voice as he tried to impress upon her that time was running out.

"I know," she said. "But I'm right in the middle of things here."

"What things?"

"School and work, mostly," she answered.

Before Hank could pick up on her comment and start applying more pressure, she asked, "How's the family? How are Emily and Brad doing? And how about the rest of the Watson kids, especially Carrie? And tell me about Rose."

"They're all fine, Roz," he said somewhat impatiently. "And not to beat a dead horse, but they all want you to come out and stay with us while you finish your degree at BYU."

Hank realized that he had laid it on a little heavily. He didn't want to burn her out on the whole idea.

"Well, I'd better go, and let you get back to what you were doing. Just don't forget, fall is closer than you think. We love you, Roz!"

"I love you all too, Hank. Give everyone a hug. And kiss the baby for me"

"I will. Bye, Roz."

Hank was right, of course. Time was running out. But time couldn't run backwards. She knew it was not realistic. They had each traveled separate paths since then. Their relationships would never be the same as before.

In Rosalind's heart, she felt that Hank was trying to build a nest of comfort and security, without having to face the fact that Rose needed a mother. He saw her as an undemanding candidate for the platonic position he was seeking to fill.

There was a time she might have been grateful for just that much, thankful for whatever attention or affection he might offer. But she was no longer that shy, insecure teenager he used to know. On April Fool's Day, Rosalind would celebrate her twentieth birthday.

CHAPTER NINETEEN

On April first, Mark William Dobson called from Norfolk, Virginia. As soon as she picked up the phone, he began to sing, "Happy birthday, dear Rosalind. Happy birthday to you."

"How sweet, Mark! How did you know it's my birthday?"

"Don't you remember how many times my mom and I were invited over to your house for birthday cake and ice cream with you and your grandma?"

"Yes, I do. Those were the best birthday parties I ever had. In fact, they were the only birthday parties I ever had. Thank you for remembering."

"Well, I hope you have a great birthday. I'd love to talk, but I just ran down here to the phone booth on my break, and I've got to get back. Happy birthday again."

"Thank you, Mark. You've made my day! You have a good day, too. Goodbye."

"Bye, Rosalind."

Celebrating in her own way, she drove to the Grayson Cemetery to visit the Matthews plot, where Charlie and Nellie, and her grandparents, Sam and Grace, were buried. She placed flowers on each grave. But instead of sadness, she felt joy and gratitude for them.

She pondered her grandmother's frequent protestations that she didn't want to change her religion. After her recent experience of sensing her near, did that mean she had changed her mind now? Rosalind felt the Spirit strongly confirm this to her.

Soon, Grandma.

The mail had arrived by the time she got back from the cemetery. There were birthday cards from Emily and Brad and the Watson family. She hadn't shared her birthdate with the O'Connors, so she wasn't expecting anything from them. But she was shocked to find a letter from Charlene Stanford.

With trembling fingers she opened the envelope, and took out the single page with a photo wrapped inside. Studying the image of two young girls, she was amazed at the resemblance she bore to one of them.

Dear Rosalind,

Sis. Lockhart asked us to send this picture of your mother to you. Rusty's so busy with the house I said I would take care of it for us. Russell and I are so looking forward to it being finished. We hope you're doing well up there.

Come to see us when you can.

Sincerely,
Charlene

$\varphi \sim \omega$

Rosalind was sleeping soundly. When she heard the familiar soft whimpering, she struggled into her bedroom slippers and drew on her robe. She crossed the room to the white wicker changing table and pulled out a fresh diaper from the shelf.

She made the change from wet to dry, then placed the indignant baby back into the bassinet. After washing her hands in the bathroom, she headed to the kitchen to warm up a bottle. When it was ready, she returned to the nursery to pick up the crying infant again. Then she walked into the next room to sit in the rocking chair near the fireplace.

The bottle was well received, and Rosalind settled into rhythmic rocking. She closed her eyes, almost drifting back to sleep, but was alerted by the sound of cooing. She looked down at the sound, but the baby girl in her arms was still contentedly feeding.

In the semi-darkness of the room, she saw another rocking chair, and another baby, in the arms of his father, who smiled back at her in the glow of the firelight. His love radiated to her across the parlor of the river house. Rosalind comprehended the scene immediately: *Twins! John Charles and Evelyn Grace O'Connor!*

A warm feeling radiated down through her head and spread throughout her entire body. It was almost like the feeling she had had when she was given the Gift of the Holy Ghost after her baptism.

Too soon, the alarm clock dragged her to wakefulness, but the dream was still very much with her. It had seemed so real that she wished she could fall back to sleep to continue its perfect happiness.

දස්ඪ

The next day, after her shift at the Grayson College library, Rosalind went to the reference section, and began looking up Florida colleges and universities within driving distance of Adrian. She just wanted to know what was out there, what her options were.

In a few minutes, her list was complete. But before she put the book away, on a whim, she thumbed through the pages to Utah. The entry for Brigham Young University brought back good memories of her time with Emily and the Watson family. But she had already decided not to apply for a transfer to the "Y."

When she reached home, the winter sun was sinking in the west amid a cushion of fluffy clouds that were rapidly changing colors from gold, to red, to purple. She let herself in, and placed her books and purse on the foyer table. She made a step or two toward the kitchen, as if by habit. Then instead, she changed her mind, and climbed the stairs to her room.

She sat at her desk, took out some pages of stationery, and began a letter to Emily and Brad.

Dear Emily:

You and Brad and Hank have been on my mind a lot lately. I want to thank you and your family for everything.

I guess everyone is still in suspense about my transferring out to BYU. It's probably my fault for not being clearer. It is a lovely idea, creating new memories with we three, you and Hank and I, not to mention adding Brad as a fourth member of the gang.

But it's always been about our high school trio, and when I try to recreate it in my mind, it just doesn't work.

Our lives have taken different directions. I've realized that we really can't just pick up where we left off. We've all grown up. That sounds strange, but it's true.

You and Brad are beginning a new family, a new adventure. In time, there will be little ones, and being a wife and mother will consume you.

I believe the same is true for Hank and little Rose. He has so much to work out in his own mind and heart, but 'it is not good for man to be alone.' Hank will find someone to make him happy again. He needs to find that one person who can make it come true, and with whom he will develop a new life.

I hope you'll understand. I'm not ending our friendship. You're like my sister, and your family is like my family. I want you to live a happy life, but I have to live mine as well. We'll always be close, and wherever we end up, I hope we can visit often.

She signed the letter and slipped it into an envelope. Then she began to write another. This one, to Hank, would be much more difficult.

∽✦∼

In early May, she received a letter from Evelyn, full of exciting news about the progress on the river house. Rusty had hired workmen to restore the original wooden flooring. There were new area rugs in high-traffic areas.

Evelyn said she had picked out drapes for all of the rooms. The front porch had four new wooden rockers, a glider and, of course, a new porch swing.

Rusty's affinity for restoration went only so far, Evelyn explained. The bathroom had been remodeled. He had added a walk-in shower, which would make it easier for him to get in and out. But he had kept the deep, claw-footed bathtub. The long pull-chain tank and toilet had been removed and sold to an antique store downtown. A modern toilet and fixtures had been installed in place of the old ones.

"You'll also like what Rusty has done with the back of the house. A new door has been cut into the wall of the master bedroom, giving it a nice, new private bath that was built on half the old back porch.

"He has also modernized the kitchen with a new sink, range and refrigerator. The icebox has gone the way of the old toilet, and is on display at the antique store. The interior walls have all been repainted, and he says that the front bedroom will be used as an office and library."

Rosalind's excitement grew as she read Evelyn's words describing each improvement. She smiled at the description of Rusty's latest project: repairing the barn and fixing up the corral.

The back of the property was fenced off from the orange grove, and enclosed a nice pasture. It would be the perfect home for Sunny Girl's new foal.

"All of this may seem extravagant," Evelyn continued. "It is expensive. But Rusty holds a half-interest in the orange groves, and will continue to receive profits from the sale of the fruit. He also has some money in his savings account, and in savings bonds.

"Since he lives at home, he has been able to get by on his disability income and his job with the newspaper. Also, since the river place is still ours, we've insisted on covering half the remodeling expenses. Someday, we will give it to Rusty as a wedding gift for him and his bride."

Evelyn didn't mention in her letter what Charlene thought of it all. On the last page, she wrote about John's new interest in pursuing his family tree.

"I think your search for your family down here in Adrian has been his inspiration. He's been writing to surviving relatives for information. And you'll appreciate this. He is spending a lot of his time in nearby libraries that have genealogical holdings for Ohio.

"Through his correspondence with a first cousin, he's been able to get a handwritten transcript of the old O'Connor family Bible, dating back to his immigrant ancestor Rowan O'Connor, from Derry, Ireland. This cousin also sent a large, hand-copied pedigree chart that shows both the O'Connor side of the family, and the Russell lineage of John's mother's people.

"Since I tag along on these excursions when I have time, I've decided to look into my own genealogy. Records are plentiful and close at hand for my ancestors who pioneered in the Tampa area in the 1840s. Now, I'm developing that family line back to colonial New England."

Rosalind was overjoyed that they all shared a love for family history. She planned to write back that she looked forward to doing research together the next time she made it down to Adrian.

And just when might that be?

❧

Rosalind was surprised when she was released from her nursery calling at church. She would miss her little ones, but agreed it was time for a change. The Bishop then issued a call to her to attend the new genealogy class being taught during Sunday School.

The Church of Jesus Christ of Latter-day Saints was making great strides in gathering valuable records and sources. In 1938, microfilming had begun, as teams visited courthouses and libraries across the country, filming censuses and court records, and often giving a copy of the reel to those making them available. As teams worked with local libraries, archives and museums, the public was sometimes invited to bring in their family Bibles to be filmed for posterity.

In the class, Rosalind learned the difference between primary and secondary sources, and what types of records were available to the public. She was already familiar with some of those, so she felt comfortable when the teacher asked her to take a few minutes one Sunday morning to describe her own research experiences. Genealogy was becoming her passion, and she loved to share the stories of her finds.

The semester would be over at the end of May. Now that her feelings for Hank had devolved into a deep friendship, they no longer threatened her future. There were only two men in her life now: the Rusty she loved, and the Rusty he might become. It was all up to him.

❦

"He sure is a beauty!" Paul said proudly.

Rusty watched the newborn colt struggle to stand on wobbly legs. His still wet coat looked darker than it was. His sire was black, but he would be a chestnut like his dam, Sunny Girl. And when he was older he would graze on the rich pasture grass at the river house.

Paul stepped back and snapped a photo with his Polaroid camera, then handed it to Rusty.

"Thanks, Paul." He grinned. "This one's for Rosalind."

She received the picture on the third Saturday in May, Armed Forces Day. He had written a note on the back,

Riding off into the sunset together.
What shall we call him?
All our love,
Rusty."

❦

Rosalind realized, that before, and if, she accepted his proposal, there were some important things to consider. What would she do with her house in Grayson, and with all her grandmother's furnishings?

There were some things she didn't want to give up. She stood in the dining room, running her hand across the smooth surface of the mahogany table, surrounded by eight matching chairs with needlepoint cushions that her grandmother had stitched. Perhaps Rusty wouldn't mind if she brought these.

During an afternoon project of walking through the house, she made notes of what smaller items she wanted to keep. On her list was the small vase on the piano that had once held torn bits of a postcard of the Salt Lake Temple with the last message from her dad. She would also keep her father's boyhood ice cream dish that had been glued back together after being broken many years before. As for the house itself, she didn't necessarily have to sell it. Perhaps she could rent it for a while.

Then there were the logistics of being married in the temple, versus being married in a civil ceremony first, and then traveling to the temple to be sealed later. Rosalind really wanted a temple wedding like Emily had had. She particularly wanted it to be performed in the Salt Lake Temple, where as a baby, she had been sealed to her parents, Charlie and Nellie Matthews.

She took out an old atlas from her Grandfather's bookshelf, and looked up the distance to Salt Lake City. It was over 2,300 miles from Adrian, and about 1,900 miles from Grayson. The only reasonable plan was for them to fly out separately, she from South Carolina, and Rusty from Florida.

But her only contacts in Utah were the Watson Family. How would Rusty feel about that, knowing her history with them? Would he mind?

And what about his parents? Wouldn't they be hurt if they were unable to attend their son's wedding?

How she wished there were a Mormon Temple in the Eastern United States. And even more, how she wished John and Evelyn O'Connor were members of the LDS

Church. She smiled at the thought that if Charlene had her way, they already were, or soon would be.

CHAPTER TWENTY

One Saturday morning in early May, Rusty stopped by the museum to visit Miss Leonard and pay his respects. He gazed at the newly hung photos of Col. Wesley Martin and the colonel's pocket watch. It made him feel closer to Rosalind, though they were miles apart.

The elderly woman leaned heavily on her cane and watched him intently. "You love her very much," she observed wisely.

"Does it show?" He felt embarrassed.

"Yes, Russell, it does," she said with a gentle smile. "Have you told her?" She walked carefully back to her desk and sat down.

He followed her like a boy going to the principal's office, and took a seat in front of her large desk. Since Miss Leonard had raised the question of his feelings for Rosalind, Rusty found it easier to talk to her.

"I've asked her to marry me," he said, looking down at his baseball cap in his hands. "She said she would give me her answer at the end of the semester."

"She still has two more years of college. But she thinks she might like to go on for her masters' degree, and become a librarian.

"There's the age difference though. I'm almost five years older, and that's a long time to wait." He wrinkled his brow and twisted the cap in his hands nervously.

"There are some jobs in the library field that don't require an MLS," she offered. "Didn't she substitute last summer for her college librarian who went back to complete her master's?"

"Yes ma'am," he answered.

"It's a goal she could pursue later if she wanted to. There are plenty of schools within easy driving distance of Adrian, where she could complete her Bachelor's degree."

Rusty perked up at the possibilities she mentioned.

Miss Leonard looked sternly at the young man sitting before her, and spoke softly. "I'm about to share something with you that I haven't told anyone else."

"Of course, ma'am." He gave her a serious look of trust and assurance.

"Organizing this museum has been a joy for me these past few years. But it's getting to be more than I can handle at my age."

He could see how difficult it was for her to admit that.

"I need to find someone who will continue this work with the right amount of dedication it deserves. I believe your Rosalind would do that.

"I could train her, and when the time felt right, I could turn it over to her, and she could run it. It wouldn't pay very much. Our funding comes from donations. But she would have the flexibility to work her hours around her classes until she graduated.

"This museum has been the love of my life, and I would like to leave it in good hands. She's very special, that girl of yours." She smiled her approval.

"Yes, she is." Grinning happily, Rusty rose and shook her hand gently. "Thank you, Miss Leonard. Thanks for everything."

He left that day feeling a lot more positive about the future, and stopped by the post office on his way home. He had something special to mail to Grayson.

∞∞

When Rosalind returned home after work one day, she found a long white envelope with the Adrian *Herald* business address among the bills and advertisements. It was postmarked May 3, 1970. She opened it and unfolded the single page inside, started to read it, then stopped, and began again more slowly.

It was a photocopy of the Line of Priesthood Authority for Russell O'Connor. He had become an Elder! A photo showed him with his bishop and other men whom she recognized from the Tampa Ward. On the back were written their names and the date, April 27, 1970.

Three weeks later she received a fat letter from Evelyn. Rosalind made herself wait to open it until after she took her last two exams.

With that burden lifted, she stood at the foyer table, and ripped open the envelope with pleasure and anticipation. She hadn't heard a word from Rusty's mom for several weeks, which was very unusual.

If she had expected a newsy letter, she was mistaken. It was just a blank sheet of paper, hastily folded over some photos.

Rosalind gasped when she saw the picture on top of the stack. There were John, Evelyn and Rusty in white baptismal clothing standing in the hall of the Tampa Ward chapel. She quickly turned it over and read the date on the back, May 18, 1970.

The next one showed John and Evelyn, with Rusty and Charlene, and little Russell.

She did it, just like she said she would. Charlene got them baptized. Rusty's parents have joined the Mormon Church!

Rosalind choked back a sob at the implication. She was happy for them, of course. But did the photos mean that she had waited too long? Had Charlene replaced her in the O'Connor family? And what about Rusty? *Hadn't he promised to wait for her answer?*

Tearfully, she shuffled through the rest of the photos, stopping when she came to the last one. There were Charlene and Russell standing with a tall, handsome man she didn't recognize.

She turned the picture over, searching for an explanation. The inscription on the back read, "Charlene with her fiancé, Richard Hanson, a lawyer from Panguitch, Utah, who moved into the ward several months ago." The look on Charlene's face answered all her questions but one.

The next day's mail brought a small business envelope addressed in Rusty's uneven handwriting. She sat on the couch, and forced herself to sort through the other mail before opening it.

Her fingers trembled as she took out a sheet of yellow-lined paper ripped jaggedly from a legal pad. The short, hastily scrawled message read:

> *Dear Rosalind,*
> *I KNOW!*

Looking forward to hearing from you.

      All My Love,
      Rusty

That night, Rosalind lay awake for a long time considering how she should answer Rusty's note. She could write him a letter, but that was too impersonal. A phone call then? No. She would go to Adrian and give Rusty her answer face-to-face.

The next morning before leaving for work, she picked up the receiver on the kitchen phone, and dialed the O'Connor home in Adrian.

On the second ring, a familiar voice answered.

"Hello. You've reached the home of the O'Connors. This is Evelyn speaking."

"Mrs. O'Connor," Rosalind said. "How are . . ."

Before she could even finish her greeting, Evelyn exclaimed, "Rosalind, dear. We were just talking about you at breakfast. It's so good to hear from you!"

"I've really missed you all. Are you alone?"

"Rusty has already gone to work, but John is out back puttering around. Is anything wrong?"

"No. I'm fine," said Rosalind. "I was just wondering if I could come down for a short visit. Would you have a spare bedroom for a couple of days next week?"

"There's always a room for you, dear! When are you coming?"

"I'll need to make arrangements. If I can get a flight, would next Thursday be okay? Is it too much to ask if you could pick me up at the Tampa airport?"

"Of course we can! That would be grand! I can't wait to tell Rusty and John! Call us as soon as you know your schedule, and we'll be there to meet you. I'm going to call Rusty right now."

"Thanks, Mrs. O'Connor. I'll call you soon. Give everyone a hug for me. Bye."

Rosalind immediately called to book her flight. Her plane would leave at noon on Thursday, and she would return Sunday evening. It was a perfect schedule. She had just finished her classes for the semester and would only have to miss two days of work. Now, all that remained, was to clear those two days off with the librarian, and call Evelyn back to confirm that she would be arriving at 2:40 P.M. Thursday afternoon.

∾

Rosalind had become at ease with traveling by air and enjoyed the short flight to Tampa. As she stepped inside the terminal, she was pleasantly surprised to see all three of the O'Connors, John, Evelyn, and Rusty, waiting for her. John retrieved her suitcase, and they made their way to the car. Within a few minutes, they were on the highway to Adrian, with the two men in the front seat, and the two ladies in back.

The topics of conversation were scattered as they drove along, though Rosalind felt the tangible curiosity about her trip. But she had come to see Rusty, and she would discuss it with him when the time was right.

"I didn't expect to see you until tonight, Rusty."

"Disappointed?" he asked playfully.

"No. But how did you get time off from work?"

"I told the boss I wanted to cover the arrival of a VIP at

the airport," Rusty said with mock seriousness.

"You didn't," Rosalind said in the same droll tone.

"So how are things in Grayson?" John asked.

"I just finished the spring semester of my sophomore year," Rosalind said with satisfaction.

"Are you taking any classes during the summer?" Evelyn asked.

"I'm not sure yet. If not, I guess I'll just work at the library until the fall."

Disappointed, Rusty asked, "You're going to work through the whole summer?"

Before Rosalind could reply, Evelyn intervened. "Well, we're just happy to have you with us, even if it's only for a few days." She reached over and patted her hand. "Are you hungry? I have dinner ready to put in the oven when we get home."

❧ ❧

After Rosalind had dropped off her things in her room and freshened up, she walked down the familiar hall to the kitchen. Rusty and his dad were watching television in the den. She stopped at the door and said, "There they are. My two favorite men in the whole world."

"Come on in," John said. "We're just sort of waiting for something interesting to come on."

"Thanks for the invitation," she said, "but I smell good things going on in the kitchen. I'll see you guys later."

"Dinner's almost ready," Evelyn called from the kitchen. "Rosalind and I'll visit while you two watch TV."

Rosalind closed her eyes and breathed in the tempting aromas of a pork roast, mashed potatoes, and vegetables.

Yes, this is home.

She walked over to where Evelyn was taking the roast out of the oven, and offered, "How can I help?"

"You can take the potatoes and veggies to the table. Oh, and the rolls. They're in the basket on the counter over there."

John and Rusty wandered in from the den. Rosalind smiled broadly at them and said, "Between good food and TV, there's no competition, is there?"

Rusty held Rosalind's chair for her, as John did the same for Evelyn. "Let's hold hands and bless this good food," he said.

After the prayer, John carved the roast. Amid good-natured conversation and hearty appetites, the dinner was soon finished. Evelyn went to the oven, and brought out Rosalind's favorite dessert, a pecan pie that she had baked for the occasion.

"Ah, another recipe you need to share with me. I'm not going to ask how you knew it's my favorite," Rosalind laughed.

"Hey, Mom, I thought you baked it for me!" Rusty exclaimed.

After the pie was finished, Rosalind stood and began clearing the table and preparing to wash the dishes.

"Mom," Rusty said. "May I borrow your kitchen help? I'd like to take Rosalind for a drive."

"Of course. She's our guest. You two go ahead. We'll visit when you get back."

❦

Rusty steered the Beast across town without revealing the destination to Rosalind. Her curiosity was almost uncontrollable. "Where are we going?" she wanted to know.

"You'll see. But don't worry, you'll recognize it."

They were soon heading through pastures dotted with lazily grazing cattle. Just as Rosalind was about to venture a guess about their destination, Rusty turned right onto an unpaved road leading between two tall, white flag poles, one flying the American flag, the other a Marine Corps flag.

"Now do you remember the way?" Rusty asked.

"Of course I do. We're going to see Sunny Girl and her foal. Right?"

The colt chased his mother around the paddock waving his brush of a tail. Rusty pulled over beside the white fence, and sat quietly behind the steering wheel, admiring the scene. Since the colt's birth, he had come here almost daily at the end of his workday to think of the future.

"He's beautiful!" Rosalind exclaimed. "Do you think he'll come to us?" She opened her door and jumped out before Rusty could be the gentleman and come around to open it for her.

They leaned on the fence for a while watching the colt cavorting with his mother.

"Have you thought of a name for him?" she asked.

"I thought we would pick one together." He turned to kiss her forehead.

"Well, don't you have any suggestions? You've known him longer than I have," she countered.

A breeze was picking up, and the Florida sun reddened low in the sky. Rusty put his arm around her waist as they watched it sink into the glowing clouds.

"How about 'Sunset'?" she suggested.

Rusty picked up on it immediately, "As in 'riding off into the sunset?' I like it. If fits." He smiled and kissed her cheek.

The colt had edged closer to them. He stuck his head through the rails of the fence, and curiously nudged Rosalind's leg.

"It's a winner," she said. "I think he likes it, too."

Rusty smiled at her happily. "Now I have something else to show you," he said as he clasped her hand.

They headed back to the pickup and he opened her door. When Rusty turned the Beast back onto the road in front of Paul's ranch, Rosalind had no doubt where they were going. They were soon on the river road, and a short while later, they stopped in front of the old river house that Rusty had been working so hard to restore for several months.

The sun had dropped below the horizon, and twilight was darkening. A light on the porch indicated that the power was on. He came around and opened Rosalind's door, took her hand, and helped her out of the cab.

"I'm sorry you can't tell much about the outside," he said, "but I think you'll like what we've done with the interior."

Rusty unlocked the front door and let her inside. The refinished floors, area rugs and curtains gave the house a charming, homey feeling. The built-in bookshelves in the front bedroom had been sanded and stained.

Though other areas had been carefully restored, the kitchen and bathrooms were a shining marvel of modernity, just as Evelyn had written.

"It's so beautiful, Rusty!" she said approvingly. "You've done a wonderful job. It's even better than I imagined it would be."

"Thank you, ma'am. I'm glad you approve," he said, as they retraced their steps down the hall to the parlor. They stood before the fireplace for a few moments. Then Rosalind took his hands in hers.

"There's something I need to tell you, Rusty."

"Is this like the answer to a question?" he asked. "Or is it more like a story that I'm not going to like?" Rusty let go of her hands, a worried look on his brow.

CHAPTER TWENTY-ONE

"Just hear me out, please," she asked with pleading in her voice. "I've kept some things to myself, but I want to tell you about them now.

"Right after I got back to Grayson from spending Thanksgiving down here, I got a phone call from Emily."

Rusty stiffened with apprehension. He feared where this was going.

"Hank's wife, Crystal, had gone into labor early, and she developed complications. She died after delivering their baby girl."

Rusty was shocked, unable to find a proper response.

"While I was there for the wedding, I was able to help out with the baby. She is so sweet, Rusty. Her name is Emily Rose."

"Emily *Rose?*" Rusty asked with a raised eyebrow. But Rosalind didn't notice the implication.

"Hank was in terrible shape, as you can imagine. One night as I sat up rocking Rose after feeding her, he came into the living room, and we talked for a while. He was so overcome with grief, that he hadn't really had time to bond with his daughter.

"The next night, at the wedding reception, he finally held her, and fed her for the first time. I knew then that he would be all right, and I realized that my feelings for him were only friendship."

Rosalind looked earnestly into Rusty's face, but it was unreadable.

"Hank and Emily, and their parents, wanted me to transfer out to BYU because of their Library Science program. He even called me a few months later to ask if I'd made a decision. But I wrote them, and said we'd never be able to recapture those good times in high school. We had all moved on, in our own ways.

"Sometime later, back at home in Grayson, I had a dream. It felt so real. In the dream I woke up to the sound of the baby crying. I got up and changed her diaper, and fixed her a bottle. Then I took her into the other room to feed her beside the fireplace.

"I was sitting there, half asleep, and I heard the baby cooing. But when I looked down she was still feeding.

"Then, when I looked toward the sound, across the room there was another baby being rocked by his father.

"It was you, Rusty. The babies were twins, and they were ours, Rusty, yours and mine. It came to me so naturally that their names were John Charles and Evelyn Grace."

Rusty tried to absorb what she was saying. He stood there looking at her in confused silence as feelings of dread were transformed into hope. Then Rosalind spoke again.

"The dream was still on my mind when I woke up. It seemed so real. I didn't want to give it up. It was then that I realized how much I love you. I wanted us to always be together.

"That dream happened early this year. I didn't write to you about it, because I wanted to wait to see how you felt about the Church first. Then I got your note that you had gotten your answer, and I just had to see you."

"I like that dream," he said. "But there's something that comes before that." Rusty held Rosalind at arm's length, his eyes penetrating hers.

"Rosalind, on August the tenth, I'll have been a member of the Church for a year, and we can be married in the temple. Will you marry me then?"

"Yes! I will marry you, Rusty. I will," she answered joyfully.

Rusty allowed her to fall into his embrace. Holding her tightly, he whispered in her ear, "Oh, Rosalind! You won't be sorry. I promise to love you forever."

Neither wanted the moment to end. He caressed her brown curls, and tilted her head back for a kiss. Then he smiled and said, "Let's go see Mom and Dad."

They walked together to the front door. Rusty let go of her hand only long enough to lock the door behind them. Still paused on the front porch, Rosalind spoke up again.

"After that dream, I think I knew what my answer would be, even before I got your note. Still, it meant so much to me.

"But Rusty, you are a master of profound brevity! What happened to make you know without a doubt that the Gospel is true? What's the story?"

"I guess I'm just hard-headed. I really knew from the beginning. Maybe I just thought I needed a personal revelation.

"Then Russell got really sick with an ear infection and a high fever. Charlene called to ask me to come over and assist Richard in administering to him. While he blessed him, the Spirit was so strong in that room, that I felt like it was full of people.

"Afterward, I was standing out front talking with

Richard, when Charlene came to the door and told us that she had just taken Russell's temperature. It had dropped to almost normal.

"I thought about it all the way home. I was saying a silent prayer when I reached the outskirts of Adrian. Then I heard, or I thought I heard, a voice in my mind. But it was as clear as if someone were sitting right there beside me. It said, 'Now, do you believe?' As soon as I got back, I went straight to my room and wrote you that note."

John and Evelyn waited expectantly at the O'Connor home. When the couple returned, there was an agonizing period of small talk.

After a while, Rusty stood up and pulled Rosalind off the couch to stand beside him. He withdrew a small, blue velvet box from his pocket and opened it, removing a diamond solitaire engagement ring. He placed it on her finger.

"Mom and Dad, I've asked Rosalind to marry me, and she said she will." He held her hand up for them to see her ring. "Meet Sunset," he said.

"Sunset?" Evelyn asked quizzically.

"It's a sweet story." Rosalind laughed. "Rusty gave me a picture of us riding Sunny Girl in the Fourth of July parade last summer. He wrote something on the back of it about 'riding off into the sunset.'

"Last Thanksgiving when I was here, he told me Sunny Girl was going to have a foal. Then he tried to persuade me to marry him by offering it as an engagement present.

"We went out this afternoon to choose a name for Sunny Girl's colt. The sun was setting and the sky was golden. It just seemed right to name our little horse 'Sunset.' What do you think?"

John spoke first, with emotion in his voice. "Well, I think it's perfect. Don't you, Evelyn?"

He reached over and hugged his wife. Her eyes were moist with tears as she just nodded her agreement.

Then John reached out and hugged Rosalind, and pulled Rusty into the embrace. Evelyn wrapped her arms around them all. Their happiness was boundless.

All their hopes and dreams for their son could not have come to pass more auspiciously. And they could not have chosen a more perfect daughter-in-law than Rosalind Matthews. Surely, given the circumstances of their meeting, and growing to love each other, the hand of the Lord was evident.

"So what now?" John asked. "You surely want a temple wedding?"

"Of course we do, Dad," Rusty answered. "We're going to need your help to pull this off."

They sat together in the den and made plans for the summer. Rosalind would continue to work at the college library for as long as she could.

John and Evelyn agreed to fly up to South Carolina in August to help her load up the furniture and other things in a rental truck that John would drive back to Adrian, with Rosalind and Evelyn following in her car.

Then they would all fly out to Salt Lake City on Monday, August 10, the anniversary of Rusty's baptism, and be married in the temple the next day. John and Evelyn were already anticipating the chance to search for their ancestors among the records of the Genealogical Society.

CHAPTER TWENTY-TWO

The summer passed slowly for Rosalind as she continued to work at the library, and made and remade her plans. Everything seemed to fall into place.

One of her greatest concerns had been leaving her grandmother's home for a realtor to try to rent out. That was resolved with a phone call one July afternoon, from a young man who introduced himself simply as Joe Pierce.

"I've just accepted a position as the new assistant pastor at your grandmother's church, and will be moving to Grayson. I'm looking for a place for my family and me to live. Reverend Rollins tells me that you're getting married, and moving to Florida, and he thinks that you might be looking for a reliable renter for your house."

"Well, Reverend Pierce, he's correct. I have a fine older place in a really nice neighborhood. I hope it won't be too big for you, though."

"Oh, no. There's my wife and me, and our three small children. From what he said, it would be perfect for us.

"We won't be arriving in Grayson until late August. Will it be available by then? We could put down a deposit. I don't want to lose it."

"The timing is just right," Rosalind said. "The house is going to be partly furnished, though. Will that be okay?"

"That's perfect. We have very little furniture of our own. We're happy to find a partly furnished home, in a nice part of town, that's big enough for our brood."

"I'll have my realtor contact you through Reverend Rollins."

She was certain her grandmother would approve. It felt reassuring turning the house over to a nice family.

❧ ❧

Early in the morning of Thursday, August 6, Rosalind waited at the Spartanburg-Greenville airport for John and Evelyn to arrive. When they came through the gate, she waved, and hopped up and down like a cheerleader at a football game. "O'Connors," she called. "Over here."

"Hi, Rosalind," Evelyn said. "You look wonderful."

"Yes, you do," John added. "If you're anxious to get going, I've got good news. We have only one suitcase besides a carry-on each. I'll run on down to baggage claim and get the bag. You two meet me there. Okay?"

By the time the ladies arrived at the meeting place, John had the suitcase and was waiting. Thirty minutes after landing, they had picked up Rosalind's car, and were driving out of the parking lot toward Grayson. John sat in the back seat, and Evelyn sat up front beside Rosalind.

They carried on the threads of several conversations among them until they took the exit to Grayson. "We're not far from home," Rosalind said, "but I want to take you on the scenic route around town, and down to Grayson College. It's a beautiful old campus."

The downtown tour was brief, but full of nostalgia for Rosalind, as she drove past Myra's Beauty Salon where her grandmother had taken her for a new hairdo after she had arrived from Phoenix. Next door was the clothing store where they had shopped for her back-to-school wardrobe. The old drugstore where they had had lunch that day had changed hands, and had since been remodeled. She smiled remembering how she had distracted attention from the young shoplifter and his pocketful of pilfered candy.

She turned off the main drag onto an old residential street lined with large oak trees that almost formed a canopy overhead.

"I want to take you by the family plot at the cemetery," Rosalind said.

A couple of blocks further, Rosalind turned the car onto a narrow, unpaved road that took them through a wrought-iron gate and into the Grayson Cemetery. At the top of the rise, she pulled over and parked by a small plot dominated by a large stone marker that had only one word on it: "Matthews."

"Come on. I want you to meet my family."

Evelyn and John got out of the car, and followed her to where she had paused between two headstones. The inscriptions on both stones were similar, except for the dates and names. On the stone to her right was engraved "Samuel Matthews, Beloved Husband." To her left, the other stone read "Grace Wharton Matthews, Beloved Wife."

"These are my grandparents," Rosalind explained. "My grandmother is the only person buried here that I ever really knew. She changed my life by taking me in, and teaching me so much about living."

She pointed to two other headstones closest to the Matthews family marker. "There's my mother, Helen Louise Martin. I was in Adrian to learn anything I could about her when I first met you two, and Rusty.

"This is my father, Charles Andrew Matthews. Everything I know about him came from my grandmother, Grace. Now, I'm going to have a living family of my own. Still, I know all my other questions will be answered some day, when I get to meet my mother and father, and my grandfather, Sam."

Rosalind pulled out her new Bell & Howell super eight-millimeter movie camera from its case, and began filming the graves and surrounding landmarks. She wanted to be able to find everything again when she came back to visit Grayson. John took close-up photos of the inscriptions on the headstones with his German Minox, subminiature, "spy" camera he had recently bought to copy documents in his genealogical research.

❧

On Friday morning, Rosalind walked through the Matthews home with her movie camera, filming each room she wanted to remember. Thoughts of Reverend and Mrs. Pierce and their children living here gave her a sense of comfort that the old house would be a happy place once again.

"John's here with the truck," Evelyn called out from the living room.

He was backing it into the driveway, when two carloads of men and teens from the Grayson Ward arrived to help with the loading. Women from the Relief Society would come later to help with the cleaning, and getting the house in order.

Rosalind walked out onto the front porch, still filming, and welcomed the volunteers. "I hope y'all like fried chicken," she said. "That's how I'm paying you for your help after the work's done."

Realizing they were being filmed, some of the boys waved to the camera. They called out the classic phrases, "Hi, Mom!" and "We're number one!"

John introduced himself to the volunteers. "Come on in. Rosalind has taped a note to everything that's going. We should probably put the heavy pieces at the front of the truck, so they should go on first."

Only a few pieces of furniture had to be muscled onto the truck: her grandfather's roll top desk, the piano her father had played in his youth, the dining room set and hutch, her mother's trunk, and her father's study desk. The rest of the items were boxes, taped and labeled as kitchenware, books, bed linens, clothes, keepsakes, knick-knacks, and such.

Thanks to Rosalind's organization, and everyone's hard work, the truck was loaded by 10:30. Four Relief Society sisters had arrived, and were busily dusting and cleaning. The men pitched in to help with the mopping, and by 11:30 everything was done.

Rosalind went to buy several buckets of fried chicken, and sides of biscuits, coleslaw, mashed potatoes and gravy. By noon they were all standing or sitting around the small kitchen table, having a leisurely meal together.

Soon the helpers showed signs of leaving, and she announced, "Before you go I want to thank you again for all your help. Feel free to take any leftovers with you. The utilities will be turned off today."

She stood in the doorway for a round of goodbye hugs and handshakes. After they had all gone, she stood on the front porch with Rusty's parents. Evelyn put her arm around her shoulders.

"Don't be too sad, dear. You're moving to your own home, and putting down new roots, with a good man who loves you very much."

"And with a substitute mom and dad who will do everything we can to help make you two happy," John chimed in.

Rosalind smiled at them vibrantly. "Does that mean I can call you 'Mom' and 'Dad' now? 'John' and 'Evelyn' just doesn't feel right."

John laughed knowingly. "You bet!" He recognized the reference to Charlene's familiarity.

"Why don't you two ladies get your last minute stuff together, and we'll get going," he said, anxious to get on the road. The further they could get today, the shorter the drive tomorrow.

"Now, if we get separated in traffic," John reminded them, " just follow the AAA Trip Tik and you'll be alright. Evelyn's a good back seat driver, even from the front seat," he jabbed.

"We've got reservations at the Holiday Inn just on the other side of Savannah. It's a good place to spend the night. I marked it on the map for you. You can't miss it.

"Why don't we have prayer before we leave," he suggested. "Rosalind, would you offer it?"

"I'd be happy to, Dad." She tried it out for the first time. They held hands and bowed their heads as Rosalind asked a blessing on their travels. When the prayer ended, John and Evelyn descended the steps of the front porch.

"I'll be right there," Rosalind said. "I just want to take a few more minutes saying goodbye to the neighborhood."

As she stood there, memories of the house she was leaving flowed through her mind, as well as the families on the street that had played such an important part in her life. She knew she might never again see Muriel Dobson, or her son, redheaded, freckle-faced Mark William.

She took out her movie camera and captured footage of the Dobson house next door, and the house across the street that had been the home of the Watson family: Patricia and Phil Watson, Hank, Emily, Carrie, Donald, Scott, the twins Billy and Brent, and baby Adam, who had lived only a few short weeks. In her heart, those friends and loved ones would always be with her.

All the important people in her life had moved away, their houses now occupied by new neighbors. The thought of a whole neighborhood of strangers brought tears to her eyes. Now she firmly decided she could leave that all behind. On the other hand, she was comforted by the knowledge that she was only leaving Grayson, and could take her memories of former days with her.

It was time to go. As she packed the movie camera away in its padded case, John's call from the driveway interrupted her thoughts. "We're all loaded, honey. We should get on the road soon."

Rosalind joined him beside the rental truck, and smiled up at him. He wrapped her in one more comforting hug. Then he turned to his wife of thirty years, kissed her cheek, and embraced her.

"See you down the road, Sweetheart," he said tenderly as he opened her car door.

Rosalind took one last look around. Had she forgotten anything? She had given duplicate sets of house keys to Reverend Rollins to pass along to Reverend Pierce and his wife, and to the realtor. She had locked the front door with her grandmother's well-worn ring of keys, and now she dropped them into her purse, feeling a strong sense of her grandmother's presence.

"I love you, Grandma. Thank you." she said softly.

CHAPTER TWENTY-THREE

The beautiful scenery along the way was new to Rosalind and Evelyn, and they commented often on interesting sights as they drove along.

"You know, Mom, I was so happy to learn that you and Dad had joined the Church. I was so surprised by the way you made the announcement with the photos. I've wondered ever since, how did it happen? Would you be comfortable sharing your conversion story with me?"

"I didn't mean to be mysterious about it," Evelyn answered. "We saw the changes taking place in Rusty. We learned a lot by asking him questions. He explained things so well. I made friends with some of the ladies at the ward through Relief Society.

"John became interested in his family history, largely because of you and your visits to Adrian to locate your mother's family. We were all so moved by how you found your grandfather and your Aunt Sue. All those things were the beginnings.

"One evening, we were talking to Rusty about eternal marriage. Out of the blue, John told him he wanted that for us, and I wanted it too."

"So you had gained a testimony on your own, then?" asked Rosalind.

"Well, not exactly on our own. The King James Version of the Bible was already familiar to us. We had both grown up with it, and that's what we read to our sons.

"Rusty gave each of us a copy of the Book of Mormon. We read it together, and I think what really convinced us was Moroni and his testimony.

"We took his challenge to heart, and prayed to know if what we had been learning was true. I'd never had a scripture affect me so deeply. Moroni's promise that the Holy Ghost would reveal the truth to us if we asked with 'real intent' was so simple, and yet so powerful. We did ask if these things were true and as he promised, as they say, the Holy Ghost made the truth of it known to us.

"I think we really surprised Rusty when we told him we wanted to be baptized. When he got over his shock, and realized we were serious, he insisted we should have the lessons from the missionaries first."

Rosalind asked hesitantly, "Did you meet the missionaries at Charlene's apartment?"

"No. Actually, a couple of missionaries in Tampa had a car, and they drove over twice a week and taught us. We had all the lessons in just two weeks. Then one of them interviewed us after the discussions were over, and set up a date for our baptism. Rusty baptized us the next week."

Selfishly, Rosalind was relieved that they had found the Church on their own, and not just through Charlene's efforts. She chided herself at the uncharitable thought. Hopefully, none of them would ever know the petty jealousy she had felt.

Just then the realization came to her. "We'll all need to make this trip again next summer, so you and Dad can be sealed in the temple, and Rusty can be sealed to you!"

"Yes," Evelyn said through misty eyes, "for time and all eternity."

❧❧

They had managed to keep each other in sight as they drove at a steady pace toward Florida. The sun was low in the western sky when they followed the sign to turn off at the Holiday Inn just past Savannah.

John climbed down from the cab of the rental truck, and walked over to where Rosalind had parked her car. "How's everybody doing?" he asked.

"Tired," said both women almost in unison.

"If you ladies will go on over and get us checked in, I'll drive across the road to that gas station, and fill up so we'll be ready to get on the road in the morning. Then we'll go eat supper, and I'll take Rosalind's car over to gas up before we turn in for the night."

Rosalind and Evelyn were waiting for him in the foyer when he returned. "We're all checked in," Evelyn said. "Let's go to our rooms for a few minutes to freshen up, and then we'll be ready to get something to eat."

The restaurant next door was apparently a local favorite. The menu was perfect for the three weary travelers.

"I'm having breakfast for dinner," John said. "I'll have the 'Georgia Eye-Opener' with scrambled eggs, sausage, ham and pancakes. Oh, and orange juice."

"Coffee or tea?" the waitress asked.

"Suddenly, I just can't stand the stuff," he said with a wink at his wife.

Evelyn was willing to overlook John's departure from his strict low-salt, low-fat, low-cholesterol diet. This was, after all, a special occasion. She and Rosalind ordered more sensibly.

Later that Friday night, they walked back across the parking lot to the motel. John put his arm around his wife and kissed her cheek.

"I love you, sweetheart," he said tenderly.

"I love you too, honey," she put her arm around his waist.

"I don't know about you two," Rosalind smiled at them as they parted ways, "but I'm going to shower and go straight to bed. I'm setting my alarm clock for five in the morning. I'll give you a call when I'm ready to go."

Back in her room, Rosalind didn't realize how tired she was until her head hit the pillow. Yet, thoughts swirled, and she was too excited to fall asleep.

Tomorrow she would be with Rusty, and together they would make their final preparations for their trip to Utah. Her thoughts were of the doors of the Salt Lake Temple as she finally drifted off to sleep.

ဏ‑ᑐ

Rosalind's alarm clock sounded at 4:30 Saturday morning. *I thought I set that thing for five.* She moaned, and pulled herself from sleep, and knelt by the bed to say her morning prayers. She followed that with an eye-opening shower.

Lightheartedly she brushed her teeth, stopping briefly to

look at her image in the mirror. "No regrets, Roz. You're one of the happiest girls in the world!" she said out loud.

After quickly packing her small bag, she picked up the phone, and called the O'Connors' room. "Good morning," she said brightly when Evelyn answered. "I'll be all set in about ten minutes. Take your time. I'll meet you in the foyer when you're ready."

"We old folks are moving a little more slowly, but we should be ready within a half hour. Are you excited?"

"Of course! I'm so thrilled that I'll get to see Rusty today! But there's no rush. You and Dad take your time."

She hung up the phone, and thought to herself how easily it had come to her to call John O'Connor, "Dad."

After checking out of their rooms, the three of them walked across the parking lot to the restaurant next door for breakfast. Rosalind ordered waffles, and ate them with a spread of grape jam. Evelyn smiled to herself.

Within a half hour, they had finished eating, paid their check, and were on the road. With quick stops for gas along the way, and hamburgers for lunch, they made very good time. By 1:30 that afternoon, they had reached the outskirts of Adrian.

Rosalind was delighted to see the familiar sites she had come to love. With John in the lead, they drove down the main street, retracing the route of the rodeo parade. On her right was the office of the Adrian *Herald*. John drove on past the O'Connor house, and took the river road.

When they rounded the familiar curve, excitement swept over Rosalind as she sighted the house that would now be her home. A new addition caught her attention. A flagpole stood tall in the front yard, and the Stars and Stripes waved boldly.

Rusty's beat-up blue, Chevy pickup truck, was parked in the newly paved semi-circular driveway. He was here!

John pulled to a stop in front of the porch steps, and climbed stiffly out of the truck. Rusty came down the steps, and shook hands with his dad, and then threw his arms around him. Evelyn was next in line, and Rusty gave her a hug and a kiss on the cheek.

Then he turned to Rosalind. "Hey, beautiful, I've been waiting for you. What kept you?" he said as he looked into her eyes.

"I've been waiting for you too, Rusty, for a long time." He swept her into his arms and kissed her eagerly.

"I've missed you so much!" Rosalind exclaimed, clinging to him tightly.

"Okay, you two lovebirds," John said, interrupting their reunion. "Let's get this truck unloaded, so I can turn it in today. Did you get any help lined up?"

"Here's the cavalry now, and just in time." Rusty pointed out a pickup truck and a car full of friends pulling into the driveway.

John called out, "Hey, you guys. Ready to do some heavy lifting? There's an old roll-top desk in there that weighs a ton." He looked serious, but Rusty flashed an indulgent grin at his fiancé.

His friends lined up, and peered into the truck. "Well, let's get these boxes and lighter things out of the way first," Rusty said. "They can go in the back bedroom for now."

They formed a "bucket brigade" and passed the boxes up the line, across the porch, and into the house.

The student desk and Nellie's old trunk were the next things off the truck. They were taken to the front bedroom where the trunk was placed on a colorful, newly braided rag rug that Evelyn had made.

Then came the dining room table, chairs and hutch. The piano was much lighter and more maneuverable. The guys placed it on the north wall of the parlor. That just left the old roll top desk.

"You're right," Paul said. "I'd say it weighs at least a ton! It's as big as a tank!"

It took four hefty guys and much effort to wrestle it down from the truck, onto a dolly, and up the wooden ramp they had laid across the porch steps. Once they reached the front doors, they set it down an old quilt on the refinished floors so they could move it into the office off to the left. Positioning it on the front wall behind the porch, they eased it off the quilt and dolly, one corner at a time.

"That desk will be there permanently," Rusty declared. "The next time there's heavy stuff to move, I'll be on my way to the cemetery, and somebody else can do the lifting."

"Well, that's a day's work in itself," said one of Rusty's friends. "How did you get it onto the truck in the first place?" he asked Rusty's dad.

"Levitation," John called from across the room. "It's an old Navy trick."

"Well, why didn't you . . .?"

"Don't ask," he answered the unfinished question. "I can only use it once."

❧

It was a hot, humid day, so as soon as the work was finished, Paul and his friends stripped down to swimming trunks. They ran whooping across the river road to the dock, and jumped into the water to cool off. While they swam, Evelyn drove Rosalind's car to pick up some pizzas and soft drinks.

When she returned, Rusty's friends were sitting around on the porch in their damp clothes. They finished off the pizzas and drinks in short order.

Afterward, Paul stood and grabbed Rusty in a manly hug. "Thanks for the pizza, man. We're getting out of here before you think of something else to haul into this house."

The other guys agreed loudly, and filed by to thank Mrs. O'Connor for the meal, and to give Rusty a strong handshake. Then they piled into the two vehicles.

Paul called back from his truck before they drove away, "Call us again if you need anything—next year!" Then they sped off down the river road in a cloud of dust.

John was anxious to bring the workday to a close. "Rusty, I'm going to go turn in the truck. I need you to follow me over, and give me a ride home. You know where the truck rental place is, don't you?"

"Yes sir. You go on ahead. I'll be there by the time you finish the paper work."

John called out to Evelyn to tell her they were leaving. "I'll see you at home, Sweetheart! You and Rosalind take your time."

"Okay. We're just going to look through the house first. We'll be on home in a little bit," she answered.

After checking to see that the labeled boxes had been correctly dispersed, they walked back through the house to the largest bedroom that would be Rosalind and Rusty's. The new master bathroom that had been built onto the back porch was entered privately from the bedroom. A new double bed, with a couple of easy chairs and bedside tables on either side gave the room a relaxed atmosphere.

"I hope you like the drapes I picked out," Evelyn said. "I didn't know what color scheme you would prefer, so I stayed with the neutral ecru. Of course, you can change them if you like."

"Oh, I love them! They're just what I would have chosen myself."

Rosalind looked around the large room, and tried to picture sharing it with Rusty. A strange feeling came over her as she contemplated being a married woman, and all that it entailed. But Evelyn was speaking again.

"Since you'll be staying with us until after our trip, we can wait until we get back to start moving Rusty's furniture in. Do you want to head on over to the house now?"

"Yes. I'm ready to settle in for the evening," Rosalind said. She parted the lace curtains on the parlor window to look out at the view before leaving.

∽◦≪

Though the back seat and trunk of Rosalind's car were filled with her clothing and other belongings, she had packed a small bag with all she would need for overnight.

After John and Rusty had had a chance to clean up, the tired but happy foursome sat at the kitchen table for a supper of good old Southern barbecue. They clasped hands, and Evelyn asked the blessing on the food, giving thanks for their safe return, and the helpful service of their friends.

After dinner, they all relaxed on the front porch before turning in for the night. Rosalind nestled close to Rusty's side as they sat in the swing. He reached his arm around her and entwined his fingers in her brown curls. She had never known such peace.

After a while, John announced, "I don't know about the rest of you, but I firmly intend to sleep in tomorrow morning—until at least nine o'clock."

"Well, I'll try not to wake you when I leave," Rusty said enviously. "I'm a working man, and I have a job to go to." He kissed Rosalind's nose playfully.

"Don't worry about us girls," Evelyn interjected. "We'll be busy unloading Rosalind's car over at the house," she said pointedly.

"Oh, all right," John said in surrender. "Wake me up by eight."

"Thank you, dear." She kissed her husband's cheek. "I'm going in now."

"Me too," John said, following her toward the door.

Rusty held up Rosalind's hand, studying the diamond ring on her finger. It sparkled in the moonlight.

"You know, this courtship was the toughest battle I've ever waged," he said with a smile of satisfaction. Then he spoke humbly, "This time next week we'll be married for time and all eternity."

"'Together forever,' just like the inscription on my grandfather's watch," she said looking into his eyes. Then she laid her head on his shoulder, and snuggled closer.

"Thank you, Rusty. This is everything I've ever dreamed of. I love you so much."

"I love you too, Rosalind." He stroked her cheek. "And this is just the beginning.

"One day we'll sit in the rockers on the porch out at our river house, and talk about how our twins have grown up, and moved on to new lives, just like we did."

"Yes, and don't forget our other kids," Rosalind said hopefully, as she turned to look up at him with a smile.

"Yeah, right," he answered with a grin.

She closed her eyes and took Rusty's hand in hers, and raised it to her cheek. She visualized the setting of a future sun, the river house porch bathed in a golden summer glow. Their future seemed to expand, as though it were already their history, their history of a long and happy, eternal marriage.

"Rusty," she said, "I've finally found my special place. It will always be here with you. I'm looking forward to our marriage in the Salt Lake Temple, but I already know what our life will be like. We'll grow old together in the river house, and our children will make our lives more complete."

"I've had that same dream," he replied, "and our sealing in the temple will only confirm it."

Rosalind was quiet for a few minutes. Rusty put his arms around her, and held her close.

"So this is what it will feel like to have roots," she said dreamily. "I understand now. All these years, I've been coming home to the river house, and you."

ABOUT THE AUTHORS

MARY-HELEN FOXX has been retired from a long career in public education with the Peoria Unified School District where she worked primarily in library services and IT. She has written widely on genealogical topics and has authored five books on the histories of prominent Southern families. Mary-Helen was also a contributing editor for three years with *Georgia Genealogical Magazine* and has won awards for her writing.

DANIEL FOXX is an author and historian. He is Professor Emeritus of History at Ottawa University in Phoenix and has been published in various academic and historical journals. Daniel is the author or coauthor of several historical and fictional works and also writes about his observations on life. He and Mary-Helen live in Arizona with their four sons and their families near by.

Visit Daniel's website: www.daniel-foxx.com